THE BLUNDERS

David Walliams

THE BLUNDERS

Illustrated by Adam Stower

HarperCollins *Children's Books*

First published in the United Kingdom by
HarperCollins *Children's Books* in 2023
HarperCollins *Children's Books* is a division of HarperCollins*Publishers* Ltd
1 London Bridge Street
London SE1 9GF

www.harpercollins.co.uk

HarperCollins*Publishers*
Macken House, 39/40 Mayor Street Upper
Dublin 1, D01 C9W8, Ireland

1

HB ISBN 978-0-00-830584-0
TPB ISBN 978-0-00-861439-3
PB ISBN 978-0-00-861440-9

For Alfred,

I hope this makes you laugh, as your laugh is my favourite sound in the world.

Dad x

THANK-YOUS

I WOULD LIKE TO THANK:

CALLY POPLAK
Managing Director

CHARLIE REDMAYNE
CEO

ADAM STOWER
My Illustrator

PAUL STEVENS
My Literary Agent

NICK LAKE
My Editor

VAL BRATHWAITE
Creative Director

ELORINE GRANT
Art Director

MATTHEW KELLY
Art Director

MEGAN REID
Fiction Editor

SALLY GRIFFIN
Designer

GERALDINE STROUD
PR Director

TANYA HOUGHAM
Audio Producer

ALEX COWAN
Head of Marketing

David Walliams

INTRODUCTION

MEET THE BLUNDERS.

The Blunders are the most blundersome family in the blundering history of blunderdom.

They live in a crumbling country house named Blunder Hall. It has been the family seat for hundreds of years, in the heart of the English countryside.

Paintings hang upside down, wallpaper is peeling off the walls, windows are cracked, but none of those matter. Blunder Hall is the place this family calls home.

LORD BERTIE BLUNDER

The father of the family is a classic upper-class twit. He is 5,268th in line for the throne. Bertie just needs 5,267 posh people to drop down dead and he will be KING! Not that he wants to be, for Bertie Blunder is an inventor! One such invention of his is INFLATABLE UNDERPANTS. They inflate when wet. Ideal if you fall into the sea. Not ideal if you have a little accident. Bertie believes his inventions will make his family a fortune, but sadly they end up costing his family a fortune.

Still, they love him all the same.

Lady Betsy Blunder

Betsy is Bertie's loving wife. They met twenty years ago at the Upper-class Twits' Summer Ball. The pair knocked into each other and tripped into a trifle. Once they had wiped the cream, custard and jelly from their eyes, it was love at first sight.

Like many posh people, Betsy is obsessed with horses. She is never seen out of her show-jumping outfit, clutching a riding crop and shouting, "WHOA!" There is just one teeny-weeny problem. She doesn't own a horse.

Pegasus

Pegasus is Lady Blunder's imaginary horse. As he does not exist, no illustration is necessary. Feel free to doodle here.

OLD LADY BLUNDER

Bertie's mother is in her eighties. Her favourite pastimes are shooting, shooting and shooting. She is never seen without her blunderbuss. When her husband died in a bizarre blunderbuss accident, her eldest son, Bertie, became Lord of the Hall. Bertie may assume he is head of the family but he most definitely is not.

OH NO!

Old Lady Blunder rules the roost!

Bunny Blunder

Bunny is the twelve-year-old daughter of Bertie and Betsy. With her pigtails, tutu and tap shoes, she seems like a dream child. But she can be a NIGHTMARE! Bunny is the apple of her father's eye. To Bertie, she can do no wrong. This has made her believe that she is a world-class ballet dancer, painter and Hula-Hooper, even though Bunny has never even tried any of these things. However, she is excellent at being beastly to her little brother.

BRUTUS BLUNDER

Brutus is a filthy little boy of ten. His clothes are
splattered with mud, jam, gravy, sludge and snot.
He is Bunny's little brother. Unlike his sister, Brutus
delights in all things revolting.
He digs up worms from the garden to eat.
He uses the curtains to blow his nose.
He drinks water from puddles.
However, what he delights in the most is being
beastly to his big sister.

BUTLER THE BUTLER

Butler is his surname, but Butler is also the butler. This is just as well as that way the Blunders can't forget his name. Or job. Or both. Butler is from a long line of butlers. All have had the misfortune of being butlers to the Blunders for generations.

He is ninety-nine years old but still going strong. Well, strong-ish.

CEDRIC

Cedric is the Blunders' pet ostrich. An ostrich is not a sensible pet, but then of course the Blunders are not sensible people.

Cedric's favourite pastime is pecking bottoms. More of that later.

The Baroness

The Baroness is the Blunders' battered
automobile. She is an antique Rolls-Royce.
Sadly, her engine died decades ago. Now the
Baroness is fitted with four sets of pedals.

THE MAN FROM THE BANK

The man from the bank is a little man
with a big plan. A big, bad plan to seize
Blunder Hall.

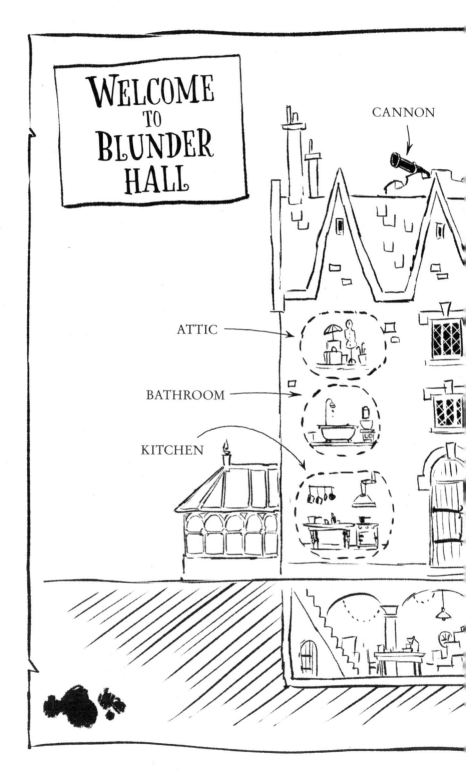

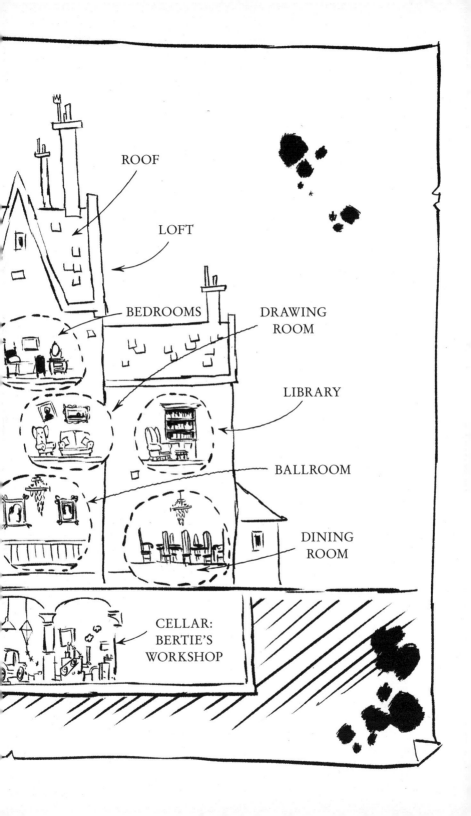

THE
TERRIBLE BUSINESS
OF THE
TERRIBLE BUSINESS

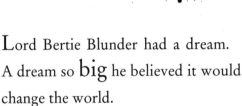

I

Lord Bertie Blunder had a dream.
A dream so big he believed it would
change the world.

Bertie spent his days inventing
inventions. Inventions that
would secure him a place
in history.

Down in the depths
of Blunder Hall, Bertie
had a workshop. Dotted
around the cellar
were his "genius"
inventions.

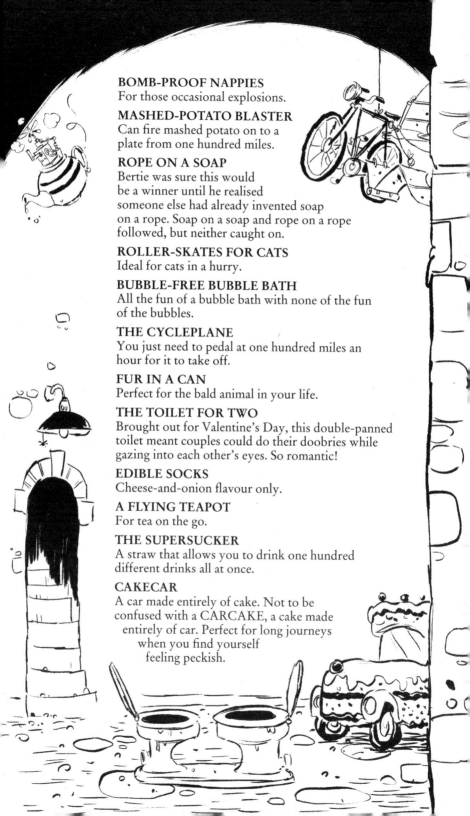

BOMB-PROOF NAPPIES
For those occasional explosions.

MASHED-POTATO BLASTER
Can fire mashed potato on to a
plate from one hundred miles.

ROPE ON A SOAP
Bertie was sure this would
be a winner until he realised
someone else had already invented soap
on a rope. Soap on a soap and rope on a rope
followed, but neither caught on.

ROLLER-SKATES FOR CATS
Ideal for cats in a hurry.

BUBBLE-FREE BUBBLE BATH
All the fun of a bubble bath with none of the fun
of the bubbles.

THE CYCLEPLANE
You just need to pedal at one hundred miles an
hour for it to take off.

FUR IN A CAN
Perfect for the bald animal in your life.

THE TOILET FOR TWO
Brought out for Valentine's Day, this double-panned
toilet meant couples could do their doobries while
gazing into each other's eyes. So romantic!

EDIBLE SOCKS
Cheese-and-onion flavour only.

A FLYING TEAPOT
For tea on the go.

THE SUPERSUCKER
A straw that allows you to drink one hundred
different drinks all at once.

CAKECAR
A car made entirely of cake. Not to be
confused with a CARCAKE, a cake made
entirely of car. Perfect for long journeys
when you find yourself
feeling peckish.

However, one day Bertie dreamed up something
so devilishly clever that he fainted at his own genius.

THONK!

II

"BEHOLD! THE UNI-SHOE! ONE SHOE THAT FITS BOTH FEET!" exclaimed Bertie.

He was standing in his workshop, showing off his latest creation to the man from the bank, his two feet squeezed into one big shoe.

"Presumably you have to be proficient at hopping," replied the man from the bank.

He was a neat and tidy little fellow, his pristine bowler hat sitting on his lap.

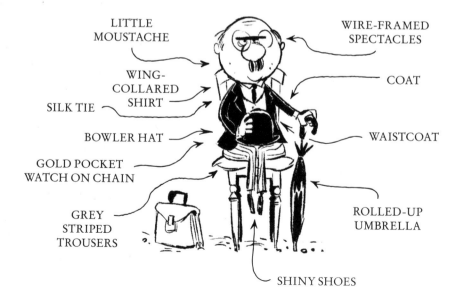

LITTLE MOUSTACHE

WIRE-FRAMED SPECTACLES

WING-COLLARED SHIRT

COAT

SILK TIE

BOWLER HAT

WAISTCOAT

GOLD POCKET WATCH ON CHAIN

GREY STRIPED TROUSERS

ROLLED-UP UMBRELLA

SHINY SHOES

Bertie couldn't have looked more different with his wild hair, moth-eaten jumper and belt made of string. For, despite being a lord and owning this great country house, Bertie had nothing much in the way of cash. In fact, just keeping Blunder Hall from falling down cost a fortune every year. That's why these inventions were so precious to him. Bertie was sure he would save the Blunders from their money problems forever.

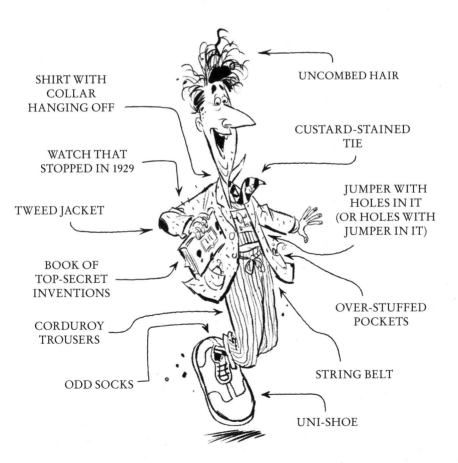

SHIRT WITH COLLAR HANGING OFF

UNCOMBED HAIR

CUSTARD-STAINED TIE

WATCH THAT STOPPED IN 1929

JUMPER WITH HOLES IN IT (OR HOLES WITH JUMPER IN IT)

TWEED JACKET

BOOK OF TOP-SECRET INVENTIONS

OVER-STUFFED POCKETS

CORDUROY TROUSERS

ODD SOCKS

STRING BELT

UNI-SHOE

"Yes. Of course, the uni-shoe wearer will need to hop rather than walk," said Bertie. "But think of all the time you'd save only having to put on one shoe in the morning rather than two!"

The man from the bank sighed. He had been pitched so many of Bertie's madcap ideas over the years, in the hope of investment from the bank, but every single one was doomed to fail.

"Let me demonstrate my uni-shoe!" With that, Bertie began bouncing round his workshop.

BOING! BOING! BOING!

He crashed into a table...

BANG!

...swept his inventions off the shelves...

THWONK!

…and landed on the man from the bank's lap.

D O O F !

"GET OFF ME, YOU FOOL!"

"Teething troubles!" replied Bertie, wobbling to his feet.

The man inspected his bowler hat, which now resembled a flat cap.

"LOOK WHAT YOU HAVE DONE!" he thundered.

"The world's first collapsible bowler hat!" said Bertie, taking it from him. "Let me de-crumple it for you."

As he tried to make things right, he made things wrong. His hand went through the top of the man's hat.

"Oops!" said Bertie, before trying to make the best of things, and placing it on the man's head. "Actually, this could catch on! The world's first open-topped hat!"

The furious little fellow got to his feet. "I have heard quite enough of this NONSENSE!"

Bertie looked downcast. "So the bank won't lend the money to make my uni-shoe a winner?"

"A winner? There is more chance of the Earth being flat!"

"Oh! I thought it was," replied Bertie.

"Good day, Blunder! Please never trouble the bank again!" said the man, heading for the stone steps.

"But the uni-shoe is my greatest invention yet!"

"It is your silliest. And that is saying something."

"It would sell billions! I could have the whole world hopping!"

"BLUNDER! YOU ARE A BUFFOON!" replied the man, now halfway up the steps.

"The uni-shoe is sure to be a SENSATION! I would bet my house on it!"

This stopped the man from the bank in his tracks.

He turned, a sinister smile on his face.

"You would bet Blunder Hall on your uni-shoe?"

"Of course! Ideas like this only come round once in a lifetime! This two-feet shoe cannot fail!" Bertie said, hopping on the spot to stop himself from toppling over.

"So Blunder Hall could belong to the bank?"

"Ha! Ha! That would never happen! This is our home! And it will be forever!"

"We'll see," muttered the man to himself as he came back down the stone staircase. He approached Bertie and reached into his briefcase.

Between the tips of his fingers were two crisp documents.

"These are the loan agreements. Standard forms. Just a formality. Please sign here and here," he said, reaching into his pocket for a gold pen. "And I will fill in the rest."

"So kind of you to save me the bother!"

"Quite!" he replied, trying to suppress his smirk.

Bertie took the pen eagerly, but held it upside down. He tried to scribble his name.

"You have the pen the wrong way up, Lord Blunder."

"Oops!" said Bertie, turning the pen the right way up, and signing his name, completely illegibly.

"And sign this duplicate copy as well, Lord Blunder, just for safety."

"Righto!" he replied, signing that one too.

"The bank will lend you the sum of ten thousand pounds for you to launch your uni-shoe business. You have one year to make it a success, or Blunder Hall will be taken by the bank."

"We will see about that!"

"Yes, we will."

"Thank you! Thank you! Thank you!" exclaimed Bertie.

He was so happy he hugged the man and lifted him off his feet.

"PUT ME DOWN, LORD BLUNDER!"

"Oops! Just a little overexcited! Oh! I can't wait

to share the good news with my fellow Blunders. They will be THRILLED!"

"Utterly," purred the man from the bank.

III

Lord Blunder built a uni-shoe factory and manufactured thousands of his two-feet shoes. However, he only ever sold one uni-shoe.

This was to a one-legged man in Belgium, who wanted to save money on having to buy a pair of shoes. However, he sent back the shoe the very next day, as it was far too big for his single foot. Bertie gave him a full refund, and that night the factory was closed down. Every penny of the ten thousand pounds the bank had loaned Bertie had been lost through his folly.

Now the man from the bank had returned to Blunder Hall, exactly a year to the minute since he'd left. He was meeting with Bertie in the drawing room. The short man perched on a tall chair, his feet not quite reaching the ground. He looked as neat and tidy as ever, a spotless new bowler hat on his head and a grin on his face.

"Blunder! Your business is bust! You have lost every last penny of the bank's loan," announced the little man. "And soon you are going to lose your home!"

"But-but-but where will us Blunders go?" spluttered Bertie, who was pacing up and down the room.

"You can all go and live in a ditch as far as I am concerned."

"How long have we got?" asked Bertie.

"Oh yes. As per our signed contract, from today, you have one month to pay off your debt in full. Then, and only then, do you get to keep the house."

"Oh dear. Oh dear. Oh dear."

"Blunder, if you do not repay the ten thousand pounds on the stroke of midnight in one month's time, the bank will seize Blunder Hall!"

"But this is our home!"

"Not for much longer!"

35

"NEVER!" said Bertie. "There must be a way to save Blunder Hall!"

The man from the bank reached into his leather briefcase and produced the loan agreement that Bertie had signed. "No. It's all here in black and white!"

"I think you are underestimating us Blunders, sir! We will not give up without a jolly good fight!"

Bertie rose from the sofa, and walked over to the door. He shouted out into the hall.

"BLUNDERS, ASSEMBLE!"

IV

One by one the Blunders breezed into the living room.

Bertie's cheerful wife, Betsy, was the first. In full riding gear, she galloped into the room, then whacked her bottom with a riding crop and cried, "WHOA THERE!"

The man from the bank looked her up and down as if she were BONKERS, which she was.

"Who are you talking to?" he demanded.

"Pegasus!" she replied with a toothy grin.

"Who's Pegasus?"

"My horse, silly! Please forgive him – he's a little flighty today. Steady, Pegasus! Steady!"

Then she kissed the air where the imaginary horse's head might be, before turning to her husband and kissing him too.

"MWAH! Sorry, darling. Should have kissed you first," she joked.

"Pegasus always comes first," replied Bertie, "except in races."

Lady Blunder turned back to the man from the bank. "Would you care to pat Pegasus?"

"NO! I AM NOT BANANAS!"

"No need to raise your voice," she replied. "You'll frighten the horse!"

Next, Brutus lolloped in. The boy looked as if he'd been thrown into a hedge, which he had. By himself. His face was filthy, his hair was a bush of leaves and twigs and he was concealing something in his hand.

"What have I done NOW?" demanded Brutus.

"I don't know – you tell me," replied his mother.

"Oh! I thought I was in trouble."

"Should you be?"

"Probably. LOOK!" He opened his hand to reveal a giant slug.

"No slugs in the house, Brutus! How many times do

you need to be told?" asked his father.

"Maybe about ten or eleven times, and then it might sink in. Anyway, it's not a slug! It's a bogey! LOOK!"

With that, he stuck the slug up one nostril.

The man from the bank tutted at this disgusting display.

"TSK! TSK! TSK!"

Brutus bounded over to him, reaching into his pocket for a creepy-crawly. "Would you like me to stick a caterpillar up your nose?"

"No thank you, boy!"

"Your loss," replied Brutus, before sticking it up his other nostril. "BOGEYS!"

Bunny was next to pirouette into the living room. She was dressed in a tutu. Humming a ballet tune, she twirled around the room, showing off like never before.

"Our little shining star!" said Bertie as he put an arm round his wife. "Can you believe she's never had a lesson?"

"I can believe," muttered the man from the bank.

The proud parents looked on as Bunny spun in the centre of the room on one foot.

"LOOK, MAMAMAMA! LOOK, PAPAPAPAPA!" she called.

"BRAVO!" they cried.

Basking in her own glory, she spun faster and faster and faster. Like a spinning top, she whirled this way and that.

WHIRL!

The smug look turned to one of panic. Bunny realised

she was spinning way out of control.

WHIRL!

She spun towards the man from the bank.

WHIRL!

"GET BACK!" he cried, flinging his head back to get out of her way.

Bunny's foot bonked the man on the nose.

BONK!

The force of the blow shot his bowler hat up into the air.

WHOOSH!

Then...

BANG!

...it was blasted to pieces.

V

Filling the door frame was Old Lady Blunder, holding her smoking blunderbuss.

"Why did you shoot my hat off?" demanded the man from the bank, squeezing his bonked nose.

"I thought it was a flying badger," she replied.

"BADGERS DON'T FLY!"

"All the more reason to shoot it! Now, who are you, you peculiar little fellow?"

"I am a bank manager. Your son..."

"Idiot son."

"Idiot son, sorry, borrowed ten thousand pounds from the bank for his uni-shoe invention."

"Terrible business!"

"It was a terrible business."

"Yes, but I mean the terrible business was a terrible business!"

The man from the bank rolled his eyes as Old Lady Blunder turned her attentions to her son.

"No more of your madcap inventions, Bertie! They will be the ruin of us Blunders."

"But—"

"NO BUTS, BOY!" snapped Old Lady Blunder before turning to the man from the bank. "So, what are you trying to tell us? And spit it out, man! I have flying badgers to hunt!"

"If the debt is not repaid, then in one month the bank will own Blunder Hall."

"WHAT? This house has been in the Blunder family for hundreds, if not millions, of years!"

"Well, soon it won't be! And here's the proof!" he said, waving the document.

Instantly, it was snatched out of his hand by an ostrich, whose neck had twisted down from behind. The bird ate the piece of paper in one gulp.

"SQUAWK!"

"Why is there an ostrich in your house?" asked the man from the bank.

"Cedric is our pet," replied Bertie, patting the big bird on its back.

"Who has a pet OSTRICH?"

"We do," said Bertie.

"Please keep Cedric well away from Pegasus, dear," added Betsy. "Last time, the bird pecked my horse's bottom, and he kicked!"

"You are all CUCKOO! COMPLETELY CUCKOO!"

said the man from the bank. "You have one month, Blunders! Not a second more. One month until Blunder Hall becomes a borstal!"

"A b-borstal?" said Betsy. "A prison for naughty children?"

"Oh, that's good," said Brutus. "I won't have to move out!"

"But the rest of us will!" said Bertie. "Moving out? It's unthinkable!"

"Nevertheless, Blunder Hall will become Blunder Borstal," said the man from the bank.

"But now that Cedric has eaten the loan agreement," began Old Lady Blunder, "Blunder Hall will remain ours! FOREVER!"

The Blunders broke into cheers. "HURRAH!"

"Do you take me for a fool?" the man from the bank snapped. "I do of course have a duplicate copy. Signed by Lord Blunder!"

The man reached into his briefcase and pulled it out.

Cedric went for that too.

"SQUAWK!"

The man tried to bat the bird away with his umbrella. "SHOO! SHOO!"

But Cedric must have been hungry.

"SQUAWK! SQUAWK! SQUAWK!"

As the man zigzagged across the living room, Cedric pecked his bottom every step of the way.

PECK! PECK! PECK!

"OUCH! OUCH! OUCH!"

With his umbrella now open and in use as a shield, the man from the bank couldn't see where he was going.

KERLANK!

He crashed straight into the butler, Butler, who stood at the door. He had been holding a silver tray laden with tea and scones.

"Afternoon tea WAS served!" said Butler, looking down at the mess on the floor.

The man from the bank's face was now covered in jam and cream. Unable to open his eyes, he cried, "LET ME OUT! LET ME OUT OF HERE!"

Still clutching the duplicate document, he tripped over a pouf...

BOFF!

...before somersaulting out of an open window.

CRUNCH!

The Blunders gathered to watch him leap into his huge Bentley automobile. The car raced off up the drive.

V R O O M !

It crashed into the bronze gates of Blunder Hall…

TWANKLE!

…before zooming off out of sight.

"He'll need to repair those gates when this place is a borstal," remarked Betsy.

"THERE WILL BE NO BORSTAL!"

thundered Old Lady Blunder.

"But he said he is going to build one," said Bunny.

"OVER HIS DEAD BODY!"

"Don't you mean 'over MY dead body', Mamamamamama?" asked Bertie.

"NO!"

"BLUNDERS!" began Bertie. "We must find ten thousand pounds, or we will lose Blunder Hall! FOREVER!"

"How much is in the piggy bank?" asked Bunny.

Butler shuffled over to the little porcelain pig on the fireplace. He rattled it before emptying it.

"Thirty pounds, five shillings, tuppence and a button."

"We'll get something for that button," said Betsy.

"Oh! And a tiddlywink!" added Butler.

"BLUNDERS!" began Bertie. "WE HAVE ONE MONTH TO SAVE OUR HOME! WE CAN ONLY DO THIS TOGETHER. AS A FAMILY. BLUNDER TO BLUNDER! WHO WILL JOIN ME IN THE BATTLE FOR BLUNDER HALL?"

"I WILL!" cried everyone, apart from Cedric, who squawked.

"SQUAWK!"

"BLUNDERS! ACTION STATIONS!"

"HURRAH!"

THE
BLUNDERS' BLUNDERING ORCHESTRA

Picture the scene.

That night, Blunder Hall was bathed in the light of the silvery moon. In the hall, a girl was sitting at the grand piano, with the poise of a professional concert pianist.

Her eyes were closed.

Her head swayed along with the music.

Her fingertips danced along the keys.

CLANG! BUNK! DOODAH!

TWONG! BONG! BING! BUNG!

THE SOUND WAS TORTURE!

You might as well take a sledgehammer to the piano.

Her father stepped slowly down the staircase in his pyjamas. He had tears in his eyes. Not tears of pain at the noise. Tears of joy.

As she hit the final bum note…

TWONGGGGGGGG!

…Bertie broke into applause.

CLAP! CLAP! CLAP!

Bunny leaped off the piano stool and ran to her father for an embrace.

He scooped her up in his arms, whisking her off her feet.

"I am a genius, aren't I, Papapapapapapapa?"

"The geniusest genius in the world!"

"And I've never even had a lesson!"

"Brilliance runs in the family! My darling, I have no doubt you will go down in history as the greatest classical pianist of all time!"

"Duh! I know that," she replied. "But that's nothing, Papapapapapapapa. Wait until you hear me sing opera!"

"You sing opera?"

"Of course!"

"I don't remember you having singing lessons."

"Don't need them! Just listen!"

Bunny wriggled out of her father's embrace and bounded back over to the piano. As she played…

DONK! BOOWANG! CLUMP! NUDUNUDUNUDUFUNK! PLOINK!

…she sang along…

"BADOODA MINKEY MOO PUDUDU HILLYPILLY FABAJUJA NONG!"

To you or me or indeed anyone whose surname is not Blunder, this sounded like COMPLETE AND UTTER GOBBLEDYGOOK.

Even Bertie looked a smidge puzzled.

Seven hours later, the opera came to a thumping climax.

"MANOONANEY WIBBLE-WOBBLE MOO!"

An emotional Bertie asked, "What language was that, my sweetness?"

"I speak a hundred different languages. So I switched from word to word. French. Italian. German. Russian. Japanese!"

"Now it all makes sense. But I must ask, Bunny –

who wrote this beautiful piece?"

"I did, Papapapapapapapa!"

"You write opera?"

"Of course. There is nothing in this world I can't do."

Bertie's eyes glowed. "With your talent, we could save Blunder Hall!"

"How?"

"People would come from all over the world to hear you play!"

"Oh, PAPAPAPAPAPAPAPA! I'm so happy I could SING!"

"Not just now! We Blunders spent all day thinking how we could come up with ten thousand pounds when the answer was staring us in the ears! You, Bunny! You are the answer to all our prayers!"

"I always knew I was a star! From the moment I was born! Before that even!"

"What could possibly go wrong?"

As it turned out, EVERYTHING.

II

The next morning, the Blunders were gathered for breakfast in the dining room. Butler was serving them all boiled eggs from a silver tray. But as soon as each egg was placed in its cup, Cedric's head popped out from under the table...

"SQUAWK!"

...and the egg was gone!

To add some drama, Bertie stood up from his chair to share his scheme to save Blunder Hall. After explaining the events of last night, he concluded, "And so, to launch Bunny's glittering music career, tonight we will host a concert on the lawn!"

"If my sister is singing, I'm going to need ostrich droppings as earplugs!" snorted Brutus.

"Papapapapapapa?" began Bunny. "If you love me like you say you do, please can you post him to Peru?"

"Children, please!" said Betsy.

"He's just jealous because I am soooooooooo talented!" exclaimed Bunny.

"I am much more talented than you!" replied Brutus.

"What's your talent, then?" she scoffed.

"I can move things with my own trumps. WATCH!"

Brutus put on the most disgusting display. He knelt on his chair and pointed his bottom at a teaspoon on the dining table.

PFFT.

W H I Z Z !

The spoon shot across the table, hit the teapot, flicked into the air and struck Bunny bang on the nose.

"ARGH!"

"TA-DAH!" exclaimed Brutus.

"Dirty smelly trumps wouldn't make a penny!"

"Would!"

"Wouldn't!"

"Would!"

"Wouldn't!"

"WOULD!"

"WOULDN'T!"

BANG!

Dust and debris fell from the ceiling.

As the cloud passed, Old Lady Blunder was revealed at the end of the dining table, holding her blunderbuss.

"ENOUGH OF THIS NONSENSE! If we want to save our home, you all need to pipe down and listen to me! Blunders! Here are your orders!"

Bertie was commanded to pedal the Rolls-Royce round all the country houses in the county with Butler strapped to the roof.

From the roof of the Rolls, Butler was ordered to advertise the concert with a loudhailer.

"A CLASSICAL MUSIC CONCERT WILL TAKE PLACE ON THE LAWN OF BLUNDER HALL TONIGHT! JUST FOUR SHILLINGS FOR A NINE-HOUR OPERA EXTRAVAGANZA!"

None of the Blunders played musical instruments. So, as there weren't any in the house, Betsy was ordered to make some. These were for the family to accompany Bunny at the grand piano.

Betsy tried her best, using bits and bobs found in the house:

- A tuba was made from an old tin bath and a snorkel.

- A harp was made from a broken picture frame and shoelaces.

- A violin was made from a battered biscuit tin and string from a kite. The bow was a wooden ruler with a rubber band tied to it.

- A xylophone was made from an ironing board with pieces of cutlery stuck to it. Two croquet mallets replaced the much softer xylophone mallets.

- A pair of cymbals was made from two saucepan lids.

Brutus was ordered to move the grand piano from the hall on to the patio for the concert. This was no easy task as the piano would have to be hoisted off the ground to be passed through the window.

The boy sniggered to himself. "TEE! HEE! HEE!"

This was a golden opportunity to cause some mischief!

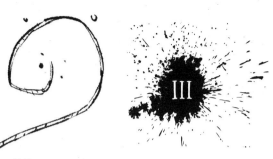

III

Under Bunny's watchful eye, Brutus went about creating a pulley-and-weights system.

First he hurled a rope over the chandelier. This chandelier was the pulley. Then he tied one end of the rope to the top of his

sister's wardrobe, which sat at the top of the staircase. The other end he tied round the grand piano in the hall. The wardrobe and the piano were the weights.

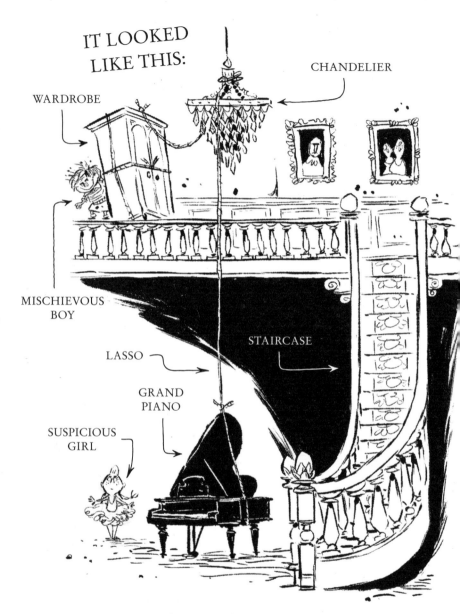

IT LOOKED
LIKE THIS:

CHANDELIER

WARDROBE

MISCHIEVOUS
BOY

LASSO

STAIRCASE

GRAND
PIANO

SUSPICIOUS
GIRL

Next came the most daring part of Brutus's wicked plan. He swung the wardrobe off the top of the staircase, before leaping on top of it.

THUNK!

Adding his weight to the wardrobe lifted the grand piano off the ground.

"CAREFUL!" ordered Bunny from below.

'Careful' was the last word you would use to describe Brutus.

The boy began swinging the wardrobe from side to side.

" F L A M I N G B A R N A C L E S ! " exclaimed Brutus. He was playing at being a pirate swinging from one ship to another.

"WHAT ARE YOU DOING, YOU BEASTLY BEAST?"

"YOU'LL SEE!"

The wardrobe smashed into the grand piano.

KERLANG!

" N O O O O ! " cried Bunny.

"ARRR!" shouted Brutus in triumph.

Then the piano bashed into a wall.

THERUNT!

"STOP!" wailed Bunny.

But her brother wasn't done yet!

He leaped off the wardrobe and on to the floor. This sent the wardrobe soaring and the piano plummeting. The wardrobe crashed into the chandelier.

BASH!

CLANK!

Both were smashed to pieces.

Meanwhile, the grand piano struck the floor at speed.

TWUNK!

It broke in two.

SNAP!

"NO!" wailed Bunny.

The grand piano was now a not-so-grand piano!

The only good thing was that it would now fit through the back door.

"REVENGE!" cried Bunny.

She leaped on her little brother and tied one end of the rope to the back of his shorts.

Next, she yanked on the other end of the rope, sending the little brute all the way up to the ceiling. He clonked his head.

DONK!

Then Bunny let go of the rope, and Brutus dropped to the floor. He bumped his bottom.

BUMPH!

This she did a hundred times.

DONK!

BUMPH!

DONK!

BUMPH!

DONK!

BUMPH!

DONK!

Bunny would have done it a hundred times more, save for her father hurrying into the hall.

"My darling daughter!" exclaimed Bertie. "Splendid news! All the upper-class twits in the county are coming to the concert tonight! We Blunders are going to make a fortune!"

Then he took in the scene of utter devastation.

"Has there been some little mishap?" he asked.

That afternoon, the Blunders assembled to rehearse for the concert.

Everyone took their places on the patio, except Betsy. She was standing on the lawn, brushing the air.

"WHAT THE BLAZES ARE YOU DOING?" demanded Old Lady Blunder.

"I am grooming Pegasus!" she replied.

"COME HERE THIS INSTANT!"

"But I haven't braided his tail yet!"

"THIS INSTANT!"

Betsy patted some air before stomping to the patio.

"Now we are all here, we can begin," said Old Lady Blunder.

Of course, the boss of the Blunders assumed the role of conductor, using her blunderbuss as a baton.

Bunny was at the front, playing what was left of the grand piano.

Sitting behind were her family, doing their best to

play the homemade instruments.

The sound they made was… MONSTROUS! PLOODANK! MOOBABOOBA! BUNTYGUNK!

Bunny sang along.

"NUNKYPLUNK! GRITTLEDO! QUOPPLEFLUP!"

Butler the butler, who had been listening to this with his fingers in his ears, made a suggestion.

"Excuse me," he began, "but I wonder if the gramophone…"

"WELL, SPIT IT OUT, MAN!" thundered Old Lady Blunder. "DON'T DILLY-DALLY! I HAVE NO TIME FOR DILLY-DALLIERS! OR, FOR THAT MATTER, DALLY-DILLIERS!"

"Ahem! I wonder if the gramophone might save the day!"

His idea was so simple it was BRILLIANT!

"The concert is

just an hour away. With your permission I can wheel the gramophone out of the music room on to the patio. There is a dusty old record of Mozart's opera *The Magic Flute*. I can put the record on, and all you Blunders can MIME along!"

"WAH!" wailed Bunny. "It's not fair! I can sing like an angel!"

"No you can't," replied Old Lady Blunder. "You sound like a strangled stoat. Well, that's a splendid idea of mine! Butler, fetch the gramophone."

Butler wheeled the wooden box out on to the patio. He concealed it under the homemade xylophone so the audience wouldn't suspect any jiggery-pokery. When he opened the lid, he made a shocking discovery.

"I regret to inform you that the gramophone has no needle."

"FIDDLESTICKS!" exclaimed Bertie.

Just then, footsteps could be heard on the gravel drive. "THE AUDIENCE ARE ARRIVING!" shrieked Betsy. "WHAT ARE WE TO DO?"

"We need something with a pointed end to take the place of the needle," said Butler.

"I know just the thing," replied Bertie.

He dashed inside the house and returned riding Cedric, their pet ostrich.

"SQUAWK!"

"You don't mean—" began Betsy.

"I do mean!" exclaimed Bertie. "This could be the very first ostrich gramophone. I will call it... the ostrophone! Exactly like a normal gramophone, except an ostrich's beak takes the place of the needle!"

The bird shook his head violently.

"And the most wonderful thing is that Cedric LOVES the idea!"

"SSSQQQUUUAAAWWWK!" went the ostrich, flapping his wings, trying in vain to fly away.

Within moments, all the lords and ladies from nearby country houses were perched on the lawn. They looked resplendent in their dinner suits and ballgowns, elegantly poised on blankets with their bottles of bubbly and overflowing picnic baskets.

The garden was a sea of upper-class **twits.**

Butler hobbled around the lawn with a tin bucket. He collected four shillings from each twit. Soon the bucket was full. Dozens of pounds! Of course it wasn't enough to save Blunder Hall just yet, but it was a start. And if tonight was a triumph Bunny could play to thousands of people next. Then tens of thousands. Tens of thousands of people meant thousands of pounds. And thousands of pounds were what the Blunders desperately needed. Ten thousand pounds, to be precise.

The sun had gone down and the sky was diamond-dusted with stars. There was magic in the air.

This promised to be a night to remember.

For all the wrong reasons.

The patio had been set up like a stage. The piano was at the centre, with seats for all the musicians behind it. The homemade instruments were set up on stands. Cedric was standing beside the xylophone. The only thing missing was the Blunders themselves. They were waiting inside Blunder Hall to make their grand entrance.

Butler shuffled on to the stage to introduce the Blunders.

"My lords, ladies and gentlemen," he began. "Welcome to Blunder Hall's first ever classical concert.

It is my great honour to introduce to you the **BLUNDER FAMILY ORCHESTRA!**"

The family trooped out on to the patio in their finest evening wear: white tie and tails for the men, ballgowns for the women.

There was polite applause as the Blunders took their places.

Bunny at the piano.

Betsy at the harp. She would have been better with a wind instrument, as her bottom was bubbling with nerves.

POP! POP! POP!

Bertie at the violin.

Brutus at the cymbals.

Butler at the tuba.

And Old Lady Blunder at the xylophone.

This was a ruse. The gramophone was hidden under it! It needed to be hand-cranked to play the record, and Old Lady Blunder was as strong as an ox.

"CEDRIC!" she hissed.

"SQUAWK!"

"SHUSH! Now get down!"

The bird bowed his head until he was out of view.

Then Old Lady Blunder made a big display of dropping one of her croquet mallets.

CLUNK!

"Oh! Silly me!" she said to the audience. "Please excuse me. I must pick up my mallet. I may be some time!"

CRACKLE!

"SQUAWK!"

CRACKLE!

Then the marvellous music of Mozart began.

The Blunders took a moment to realise that this was their cue! They had to begin or the illusion would be shattered! Bunny opened and closed her mouth like a goldfish, miming to the singing on the record, as the orchestra pretended to play.

IT WORKED!

Under the xylophone, Old Lady Blunder cranked the gramophone as Cedric's beak ran along the grooves on the record.

CRUNK!

CRACKLE!

The audience was enraptured!

Little Bunny must be a genius to sing and play piano like that. Especially as it was only half a piano.

However, as the music reached a crescendo, Old Lady Blunder became carried away with her cranking.

CRUNK! CRUNK! CRUNK!

Her arm went into overdrive, and she cranked faster and faster and faster.

CRUNK! CRUNK! CRUNK! CRUNK! CRUNK! CRUNK! CRUNK! CRUNK! CRUNK!

The Blunders and Butler did their best to keep up, but it was IMPOSSIBLE!

Bunny's "singing" was now a high-pitched squeal.

"SLOW DOWN!" shouted Butler.

But there was no stopping Old Lady Blunder!

Old Lady Blunder cranked the gramophone FASTER AND FASTER AND FASTER!

CRUNK! CRUNK! CRUNK! CRUNK! CRUNK! CRUNK! CRUNK! CRUNK! CRUNK! CRUNK! CRUNK! CRUNK!

She cranked so fast that the record spun off!

WHIZZ!

It spiralled through the air, clonking Bunny on the back of the head.

CLUNK!

"OOF!"

She was thrown off her stool into the piano!

KERUNG!

But the music was still playing!

THE GAME WAS UP!

THE BLUNDERS WERE BUSTED!

"DO YOU THINK WE ARE FOOLS?" shouted an old major with a monocle, a military moustache and a chest full of medals. This was Major Clanger of nearby Clanger Court. He was a no-nonsense fellow, and hurled a cream bun as if it were a hand-grenade.

"TAKE COVER!" cried Betsy.

The bun hit Bertie's face.

SPLAT!

In an instant, the other upper-class twits on the lawn followed his lead, hurling their picnic food at the Blunders.

SPLAT!

SPLUT!

SPLOT!

In no time, the Blunders, plus Butler and Cedric, were covered from head to toe in trifle, blancmange and lemon meringue pie.

Then the upper-class twits shouted at the Blunders.

"THIS IS A SWIZZ!"

"WE WANT OUR MONEY BACK!"

The major wrestled the bucket of cash from Butler and stomped off with it.

KERCHANG! KERCHANG! KERCHANG!

"ABANDON HALL!" he ordered.

The twits rushed after him, dipping their hands in the bucket to retrieve their coins.

Bunny was so furious she stamped her feet. "My big chance! Ruined!"

"Our big chance to save Blunder Hall ruined too," added Bertie, giving his daughter a jammy, creamy, custardy embrace.

Betsy joined in the hug, dragging her imaginary horse in with her. "Come on, Pegasus! Poor old thing got hit by a stray trifle!"

"Well, we may not have saved Blunder Hall," said Bertie, licking his chin, "but this raspberry jam is delicious!"

"MMM!" agreed the others, licking their chins too.

EXPLODING BAKED BEANS
AND OTHER
DISASTERS

Have you ever woken up to discover that all the food in your house has been eaten by an ostrich?

No?

I thought as much.

It is something that could only happen to the Blunders.

It was breakfast time, and Butler shuffled into the dining room of Blunder Hall, holding a silver tray.

"At last!" exclaimed Bunny.

"I'm starving!" added Brutus.

"So is Pegasus," said Betsy, kissing the air next to her. "Mwah!"

Old Lady Blunder smirked and turned to her son.

"How do you know which end of that horse she is kissing?" she asked.

Bertie grimaced as Betsy continued to shower kisses on her imaginary horse.

"Mwah! Mwah! Mwah!"

"What's for breakfast, Butler?" asked Brutus.

Butler put the tray down on the table.

It was empty.

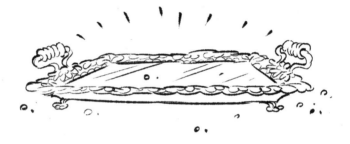

"I think you forgot the food!" said Bunny.

"Blunders," began Butler, "I have some bad news. During…"

"FOR GOODNESS' SAKE, MAN, SPIT IT OUT! WE HAVEN'T GOT ALL DAY!" boomed Old Lady Blunder.

"When I went to the kitchen this morning to prepare your breakfast, there was a scene of… devastation."

"Were we pillaged by Vikings?" barked Old Lady Blunder.

"No."

"BORING!" said Brutus.

"A FOOD FIGHT! Did the food have a punch-up?" asked Bertie.

"No. That's not how food fights work, sir," replied Butler.

"Oh. You learn something every day."

"Pegasus is innocent!" announced Betsy. "He would never do such a thing!"

"No, Mamamamama," agreed Brutus. "Because Pegasus isn't real!"

Betsy cupped her hands round where she imagined his ears might be.

"Brutus! Please! Pegasus isn't deaf!"

Butler smiled weakly. "No, the clues point to one culprit."

"Go on," said Bertie.

"The kitchen floor was covered in ostrich footprints."

Bertie thought so hard it looked as if he might pass out. "If only Sherlock Holmes was here to help crack the case!"

"IT'S CEDRIC!" bawled Bunny in frustration.

On hearing his name, the ostrich waddled into the dining room. His body was twice the size it had been yesterday. If that wasn't enough of a clue, Cedric wobbled over to Bertie and let out the longest, loudest burp.

"BOOOOUUUUURRRRRP!"

The burp was so long it can still be heard as I write this, nearly a century later.

"That's a meaty one!" remarked Bertie, wafting the air. "It's so thick you could carve it!"

"WE BLUNDERS CAN'T LIVE ON BURPS ALONE! HOWEVER MEATY!" thundered Old Lady Blunder. "THERE MUST BE SOME FOOD STILL LEFT IN THIS HOUSE!"

"Well," began Butler. "There was one thing that Cedric couldn't open. A tin that is still lurking in the lar—"

Before Butler could say "der", the Blunders had launched themselves out of their seats and were bounding to the kitchen. Brutus leaped on Cedric's back...

"SQUAWK!"

...and they got there first.

"NOT FAIR!" exclaimed Bunny, stamping her feet.

"HA! HA!"

But when Cedric's long neck reached round Brutus's back, and pecked his bottom...

PECK!

"OUCH!"

...Bunny had the last laugh!

"TEE! HEE! HEE!"

The kitchen was a mess of cardboard boxes that had been busted open, and paper bags that had been ripped to shreds.

The door to the larder was wide open. All the shelves were bare. One rusty old tin with no label was on its side on the top shelf.

"What's in that tin?" asked Betsy.

"I imagine... food," guessed Bertie.

"Oh, you are clever, darling! But I meant what kind of food?"

"A loaf of bread?"

"Papapapapa! Don't be so frightfully silly!" said Bunny. "I bet it's a banana."

"I'll wager it's a whole roast hog with all the trimmings," added Old Lady Blunder.

"Well, why don't we find out?" said Betsy. "Butler? How does one usually open a tin?"

"With a tin opener, ma'am."

"Well, there's a thing! Does Blunder Hall have one of these tin-opening thingummy jiminies?"

"Of course! Let me fetch it for you."

Butler shuffled over to the chest of drawers. The man was too slow for Old Lady Blunder.

"I am famished! I'm going to give this tin a jolly good blasting!"

Old Lady Blunder grabbed the tin from the top shelf. She held it aloft as she marched back into the dining room. Her family chased after her.

"DON'T DO ANYTHING SILLY, GRANDMAMAMAMAMA!"

"BUTLER WILL HAVE THAT TIN OPENER WITHIN THE HOUR!"

"PLEASE DON'T HURT THAT TIN!"

The lady was not for turning. She hurled the tin up into the air, raised her blunderbuss, took aim and FIRED!

BANG!

II

The tin exploded!

KABOOM!

Baked-bean bits splattered all over the dining room.
SPLUT!

All over the walls. The windows. The ceiling.
The chandelier. The butler. The ostrich. The Blunders.

"URGH!
THE INDIGNITY!"
exclaimed Bunny,
plucking pieces of baked
bean out of her hair.

Meanwhile, Brutus was licking bean sauce off the wall. "SLURP!"

"Poor Pegasus!" cried Betsy. "You are covered in bean bits! We will have to put you in the bath!"

"Grandmamamamama, you have blasted every single baked bean to bits!" said Bunny.

"What rot!" she barked. "Butler! Find me some baked beans that are still alive!"

Butler raised an eyebrow. "I will try, ma'am!"

"AND FAST, MAN! We Blunders are ravenous! Breakfast is the most important meal of the day. After lunch and dinner. And of course, elevenses and afternoon tea."

"At once, ma'am!"

The ninety-nine-year-old butler arched his body as though he was making an elaborate swallow dive. Now he could search the floor.

A curious Cedric began pecking the carpet.

"SQUAWK!"

"SHOO!" said Butler, steering him away.

The man was rewarded with a peck on his bottom.

PECK!

"OUCH!"

"BAD BIRD!" thundered
Old Lady Blunder.

Cedric waddled off to find
more bottoms to peck.

"BINGO!" exclaimed Butler.
"BEHOLD! A PERFECTLY
INTACT BAKED BEAN!"

"Jolly good show!" said Old Lady
Blunder, shooting a smug look at her granddaughter.

"We can share it!" said Bertie.

Butler raised his other eyebrow and shuffled
over to the sideboard. There he found
a sharp knife and a chopping
board. After slicing the baked
bean into five, he placed each
tiny morsel on its own bone
china plate. The chipped plates were
set down on the dining-room table. Picking up their
knives and forks, each Blunder ate their own morsel of
baked bean.

"Scrumptious!"

"So baked beany!"

"Exquisite!"

"Revolting!"

"Best one fifth of a baked bean I have ever tasted!"

There was a moment of silence. It was broken by Bertie. "I'm still hungry."

"We could always eat Butler," suggested Old Lady Blunder.

The butler replied, "I would rather you didn't."

"You could have a slice of yourself too!"

"BLUNDERS! I have a splendiferous idea!" exclaimed Betsy.

The Blunders gathered around Betsy, eager to hear.

"No, it's gone."

"Ooooooooh!"

"I know!" said Bunny. "Why don't we just buy some more food?"

There were murmurs of approval.

"We can't," replied Bertie. "I am sorry, but we don't have a penny left in the piggy bank. And we owe ten thousand pounds!"

Gloom descended on the Blunders.

"Let's not forget Blunder Hall is full of antiques," began Butler.

"We can't eat those," replied Bertie.

"No, your lordship, but you could sell them."

"Go on…"

"Not only could you fill the larder with food, but, more importantly, you could…"

"…buy a hamster?" guessed Bertie.

"NO!" cried the others. "SAVE BLUNDER HALL!"

"Oh yes," said Bertie.

"As luck would have it," continued Butler, "I read in the village newspaper of a stinking-rich American gentleman named Mr Tommy 'Gun' Torrone."

"Sounds like a lovely chap," chirped Betsy.

"Torrone is buying up hundreds of antiques from English country houses to furnish his palatial apartment in New York. Perhaps this gentleman might be tempted to purchase some pieces of Blunder history?"

"It could solve all our money problems FOREVER!" exclaimed Bertie.

"How do we find this Torrone?" asked Old Lady Blunder.

"I know the maid at Clanger Court. Mr Torrone just visited and bought every single antique in the house, including Major Clanger himself, who was snoozing in an armchair. I could telephone the maid and ask her to send Mr Torrone this way."

"YAHOO!" exclaimed Bertie. "Call her at once! RUN, MAN, RUN!"

Butler began shuffling out of the dining room, slower than a snail.

"Clanger Court is full of tat compared to Blunder Hall!" said Bertie. "This chandelier alone must be worth SQUILLIONS! It is made of the finest cut glass! LOOK!"

He clambered up on to the dining-room table, and then ran his hands along the cut glass.

CLINK! CLINK! CLINK!

"If we sell this to that Tommy fellow, the man from the bank can buzz right off!"

"HURRAH!"

As his rousing speech reached its finale, Bertie slipped on some bean sauce.

"WHOOPS!"

CATASTROPHE was about to strike!

To steady himself, Bertie grabbed hold of the chandelier.

CLINK! CLANK! CLUNK!

He began swinging wildly from side to side.

"PAPAPAPAPA!" cried Bunny and Brutus.

"BERTIE!" cried Betsy.

"LORD BLUNDER!" cried Butler.

"SQUAWK!" cried Cedric.

"BERTRAM BLUNDER!" cried his mother. "LET ME BLAST YOU DOWN!"

She raised her blunderbuss and took aim at her own son.

"MAMAMAMAMAMA! NOOOO!" he cried.

Bertie was now swinging faster than ever. So fast that the chandelier was yanked out of the ceiling.

TWANG!

Bertie was flipped up into the air. He landed on the dining-room table with a THUD.

Looking up, he saw the chandelier plunging towards him.

"ARGH!" he cried.

He rolled out of the way as the chandelier crashed on to the table.

BOOF!

Every piece of cut glass shattered.

KERPLINKERPLINKERPLINK!

The table split in half.

THWUCK!

Both sides toppled outwards.

CLONK!

As the Blunders looked on in horror, Bertie scrambled to his feet so as not to fall down the crack. But one foot went one way and the other the other.

"NOOO!"

As his legs parted, the seams of his trousers ripped.

RRRIIIIIP!

They ripped so fast that they flew off…

FLOOF!

…landing on his mother's head.

"GET THESE STINKY SLACKS OFF ME!" she thundered. "I CAN'T SEE!"

"HELP!" screamed Bertie. He was not only trouserless, but also trapped in the most painful position, doing the splits. And he couldn't do the splits.

Coming up from behind, Cedric spied a bottom begging to be pecked. He went in for the kill.

PECK!

"AAAAARRRGH!" screamed Bertie.

The shock sent him shooting up into the air…

WHOOSH!

…before he landed on top of his mother.

THOMP!

Now Bertie was stretched out across her shoulders.

"WHO IS THAT?" demanded Old Lady Blunder, her face still covered with the ripped trousers.

"IT'S ME!"

"WHO'S ME?"

"YOUR SON!"

"I SHOULD HAVE KNOWN!" she exclaimed.

It was as if they were an acrobatics act! An acrobatics act that had never done acrobatics before! Old Lady Blunder stumbled this way and that as her son went round and round on her shoulders.

"HELP!" cried Bertie.

The other Blunders and Cedric orbited them. They edged nearer, arms (or wings) outstretched to grab hold of them and slow them to a stop.

That was not to be!

Instead, Bertie's head clonked against Brutus's.

CLONK!

Brutus fell on top of Cedric.

Cedric fell on top of Bunny.

Bunny fell on top of Betsy.

"URGH!"

They were helpless to prevent Old Lady Blunder crashing into the sideboard.

THEROMP!

The crockery soared into the air…

WHOOSH! WHOOSH! WHOOSH!

…before smashing on the floor!

CHUNK! CHONK! CHANK!

The gravy boat struck a painting on its

way down.

KERCHUNK!

The painting swung sideways, hitting the next

painting as it dropped to the floor.

BOSH!

That painting hit the next…

BOSH!

…which hit the next…

BOSH!

…which hit the next.

BOSH!

It was like dominoes falling.

Despite the best efforts of Butler and the Blunders,

soon every painting had crashed to the floor.

SHONT! SHONT! SHONT!

One fell right on top of Brutus's head.

CLONK!

Bunny chortled. "HA! HA! HA!" But she soon stopped chortling as the last painting landed on her foot.

THUNT!

"OUCH!"

Bunny clutched her foot. Hopping around the house as if she were riding a pogo stick, she bounded out of the dining room into the hallway.

HOP! HOP! HOP!

There she crashed into the side tables.

BONK!

They were cluttered with antique vases and porcelain ornaments. These all took flight, before smashing against the walls, the glass and porcelain shattering on the floor.

KERANKLE!

Soon, everything of value downstairs had been destroyed in this CARNIVAL OF CALAMITIES! The upstairs would be next!

V

As the Blunders rushed out, Cedric was left alone in the dining room. Hidden in a fold of the silk curtains, he found a large clump of baked beans. In seconds, he had gobbled up the lot.

"SQUAWK!"

Instantly, the bird's tummy began to gurgle.

FUZURGLE!

Those baked beans plus all the food he had wolfed down in the night created a storm in his stomach.

A THUNDERSTORM!

Cedric blasted out a thunderous BOTTOM BANGER!

BLLLUUUUURRRP!

It was so powerful that Cedric became the first ever ostrich to take flight!

ZOOM!

Cedric looped the loop in the dining room before zooming out and up the staircase.

WHOOSH!

Like a giant feather-covered rubber ball, Cedric rebounded off the walls…

DOINK!
DOINK!
DOINK!

…taking every piece of furniture, every painting and every antique thingummy jiminy with him.

CRASH!

BANG!

WALLOP!

"Everything is ruined! RUINED!" cried Bertie.

"NOT QUITE!" said Old Lady Blunder. She brought up her blunderbuss, pointed it at the one porcelain figurine that hadn't been broken and fired.

BANG!

"There! That's everything!"

"Thank you, Mamamama," said Bertie.

Butler shuffled into the hall. "Wonderful news! I just spoke to Maid the maid on the telephone. Mr Tommy 'Gun' Torrone will stop off at Blunder Hall first thing in the morning on his way back to the Americas."

Just then Butler noticed the devastation.

"Oh. Perhaps I should tell him not to come?"

"NO!" replied Betsy. "If he likes jigsaw puzzles, then he could spend the rest of his life sticking everything back together."

"We do have one antique left in the house we could sell!" said Brutus.

"Do we?" replied Old Lady Blunder.

"Yes. YOU!"

We return to our story as Old Lady Blunder is holding her grandson upside down by his ankles.

"Sorry, Grandmamama! I didn't mean you are an antique!"

"THEN WHAT DID YOU MEAN?"

"I erm, well…"

"SPIT IT OUT, BOY!"

"Um, so, I meant you could pretend to be an antique!"

"WHAT?"

"Me too! All of us Blunders could, then we'd fool that American chappie into buying us!"

There were murmurs of approval from his fellow Blunders.

It was a preposterous plan. So preposterous that it might just work!

Sadly, no one spotted the scheme's fatal flaw.

"Should we take a moment to map the whole plan out?" suggested Butler. Something was troubling him, but he didn't know quite what just yet.

"THERE ISN'T TIME!" thundered Old Lady Blunder. "WE HAVE A FILTHY RICH AMERICAN MAN TO CON! BLUNDERS, LET'S GO TO WORK!"

"HURRAH!"

So, the Blunders put their plan into action…

The next morning, Brutus wrapped his big sister from head to toe in tin foil so she could pass as a suit of armour.

To get her revenge, Bunny stuck her brother's face through a hole in a painting. He was to be the *Mona Lisa*. She added some make-up and a wig made from a filthy mop to complete the illusion.

Old Lady Blunder decided that she would be a stone statue. That would befit her status as the head of the family. So she poured craft glue all over herself and stuck on shreds of old newspapers. This was a super idea until the papier-mâché dried, and she couldn't move a muscle.

Bertie believed he had a breakthrough with his latest invention, the very first HUMAN CUCKOO CLOCK.

"Why bother with all the clockwork parts when you can have a person hiding inside?"

He tied bits of wood from the broken furniture to his body, leaving a little hatch at the top. He put a glove on his hand, so it looked like a puppet. On the hour, every hour, Bertie pushed his hand out of the hatch and made the sound of a cuckoo.

"CUCKOO!

CUCKOO!"

The real bird of the family, Cedric, pretended to be an ostrich rug by lying face down flat on the floor.

Betsy had the most bizarre idea. She would disguise herself as a chandelier by hooking every silver Christmas decoration to herself, and then she'd dangle from the ceiling. This was the one that seemed the most DOOMED to fail.

AND TIME WAS RUNNING OUT! MR TOMMY "GUN" TORRONE WAS DUE ANY MOMENT!

Butler the butler was entrusted with welcoming this American gentleman to Blunder Hall. Then he had to do the impossible: fool him into buying all these "priceless antiques".

They truly were priceless, as no one would pay a penny for them.

Soon, the sound of an engine buzzed overhead.

BRRMMM!

Butler shuffled over to the baked-bean-splattered window. He observed a large aeroplane land on the lawn.

"He must be stinking rich!" he muttered to himself as a short, round man stepped out of the plane.

Tommy "Gun" Torrone looked like a gangster the Blunders had seen in the movies.

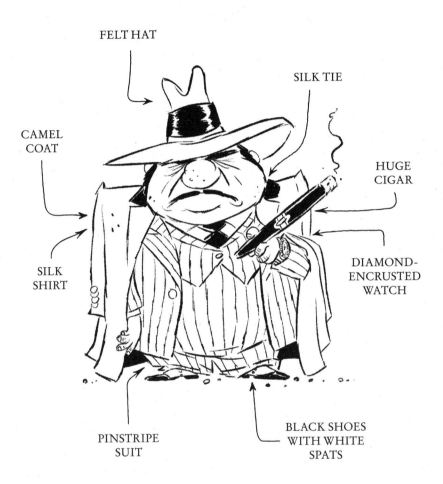

FELT HAT

SILK TIE

CAMEL
COAT

HUGE
CIGAR

SILK
SHIRT

DIAMOND-
ENCRUSTED
WATCH

PINSTRIPE
SUIT

BLACK SHOES
WITH WHITE
SPATS

The biggest clue to Torrone not being a law-abiding
citizen was the huddle of heavies who flanked him. Each
one was officially a brute.

The heavies were so menacing that Butler shuffled off

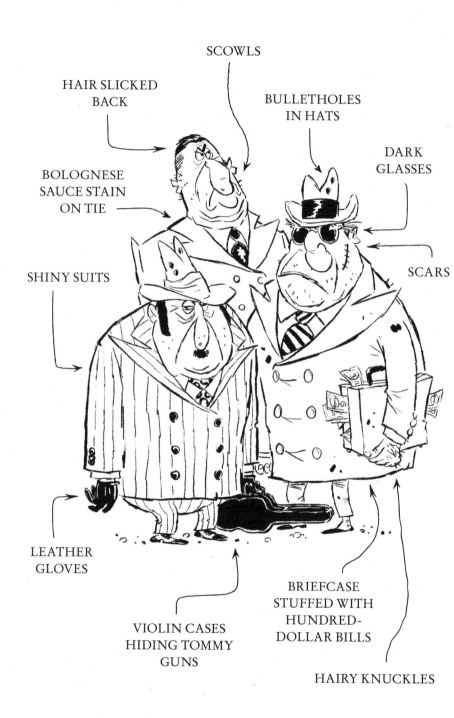

as fast as he could shuffle to hide in the larder. But before he could reach the kitchen there was a loud rap on the door.

KNOCK! KNOCK! KNOCK!

And again.

KNOCK! KNOCK! KNOCK!

And again.

KNOCK! KNOCK! KNOCK!

Butler was frozen in fear.

"OPEN THIS DOOR OR WE WILL BLAST IT OFF ITS HINGES!" came a voice from the other side.

The ancient butler took a deep breath, fixed a smile on his face and opened the door.

"Afternoon good," he said, tongue-tied with nerves.

"WHO IS THIS FOSSIL?" barked the short, round man.

The brutes behind him all laughed heartily.

"HA! HA! HA!"

"I am Butler the butler. And good afternoon to you too," replied Butler with a hint of British sarcasm.

"Wise guy, are you?" said Torrone, grabbing Butler by his lapels and lifting him off the ground.

"No! No!"

Torrone dropped him. Then he and his heavies pushed past the old man and stomped into the house.

"What a dump!" remarked Torrone.

"HA! HA! HA!" laughed the brutes.

"Let's get the heck out of this crummy place before it falls down!" said Torrone as he swept back towards the front door.

"Just one moment, Mr Torrone, sir!" said Butler.

"WHAT?"

"I do have some rather special antiques to show you. Ones you wouldn't find anywhere else in the world."

"You better be right! Or there'll be trouble!"

VIII

Butler guided the guests through to the ballroom.

There, on display, were the Blunders. They were frozen still, disguised as antiques.

"WHAT THE...?" spluttered Torrone.

"If you might indulge me, sir – this piece is worth a fortune. The suit of armour dates back to medieval times."

Bunny did her best not to rustle under the tin foil, but she had an itchy botty and couldn't help scratching it

RUSTLE!

"Did that thing just move?" asked Torrone.

"No!"

RUSTLE!

"It just moved again!"

"No, it didn't, sir!"

RUSTLE!

Torrone leaned in to Butler until they were nose to nose.

"What kind of low-down, double-crossing dirty trick are you trying to play on me?" demanded Torrone.

RUSTLE!

"IT'S HAUNTED!" said Butler.

"WHAT?"

"The suit of armour, it's haunted!"

"Who by?"

"A real-life – I mean real live ghost! The first Lord Blunder, who died in battle."

"How did he die?"

"He couldn't get out of his suit of armour. And tin openers hadn't been invented yet."

RUSTLE!

"A ghost! I could do with one of those to spook the cops! HA! HA!" Torrone chuckled.

The heavies chuckled too. They had to. They were being paid to find their boss funny.

"HA! HA! HA!"

"I'll take it!"

"A wise choice, sir," replied Butler, guiding the mob away from Bunny. "Sir! This painting needs no introduction! May I present... the *Mona Lisa*."

Brutus did his best enigmatic smile.

"Never heard of this broad!" spat Torrone.

"It's famous, boss!" said the least heavy heavy. "By Leonardo da Vinci!"

"If I want you to talk, Bozo, I'll say 'talk'!"

"Sorry, boss."

Torrone inhaled deeply on his cigar before exhaling.

The puff of smoke tickled Brutus's nose, and he sneezed.

"ATISHOO!"

The snot landed right in Torrone's face.

"What the...?"

"Do not fret, sir. They do say the *Mona Lisa* is incredibly lifelike. Its eyes, and snot, follow you around the room."

"How much is it?"

"How much have you got?"

"I like this guy!" exclaimed Torrone, playfully slapping Butler on the cheeks.

SLAP! SLAP! SLAP!

"Thank you, sir! Now, moving very swiftly on! Behold Blunder Hall's exquisite stone statue."

"What is it meant to be? A hippopotamus?"

"GRRR!" growled Old Lady Blunder from under her papier-mâché shell.

"What was that noise?" demanded Torrone.

IX

Butler had to think fast. "I believe one of your rather heavy heavies let out a trouser toot."

Torrone gave his heavies a filthy look, then turned back to the statue.

"Where would you put the great big lump?" he asked.

"GRRR!" went Old Lady Blunder again.

"That sounded like a growl!"

"These trouser toots come in all shapes and sizes, sir! And I think this statue would take pride of place in any garden!"

"I live a hundred floors up. I don't have no garden."

"Oh no, but perhaps you could use it to squash one of your rivals!"

"Ha! Ha! You old devil, Butler! I could see little Al Capone's feet sticking out from under this!"

"HA! HA!" laughed the heavies.

"I'll take it!"

"GRRR!"

"Do you ever need to tell the time, sir?" asked Butler, steering him away from the statue towards the next antique.

"Yes. But I have a watch for that!" replied Torrone, flashing his diamond-encrusted timepiece.

"Well, this is even more convenient than a wristwatch!" Butler said, presenting Bertie's pathetic attempt at a cuckoo clock.

"What the heck is this piece of garbage?" asked Torrone. In fairness to him, it did not look at all convincing.

"A cuckoo clock, sir!"

"What does it do?"

"It goes CUCKOO on the hour, every hour!"

Torrone checked his watch. "It's coming up to five o'clock now!"

"Well then, sir, it should go cuckoo!"

One of the heaviest heavies leaned in to take a closer look.

The noise of snoring was coming from inside.

"ZZZ! ZZZ! ZZZ!"

"What is that?" demanded Torrone.

"ZZZZ! ZZZZ! ZZZZ!"

"Oh! Just the inner workings of the cuckoo clock, sir!"

"ZZZZZ! ZZZZZ! ZZZZZ!"

"If it's working, why doesn't it go *cuckoo*?"

"Oh! It must have just fallen asleep, sir."

Butler thumped the clock as hard as he could.

THWUMP!

This woke up Bertie, who instantly made a "CUCKOO" sound and shot his hand out of the hatch. Not being able to see what he was doing, he biffed the heavy on the noise.

BOINK!

"OW!"

Torrone hooted with laughter.

"HA! HA! I like this!"

"I knew you would, sir!" said Butler, moving on. "Now this ostrich rug is one of a kind!"

Torrone went to step on it.

"Oh! I wouldn't do that, sir!"

"Why not?"

"Well, the rug may squawk!"

This only spurred Torrone on. He put his foot down on it.

"*SQUAWK!*"   "I did warn you, sir!"

A smile spread across Torrone's face.

"A SQUAWKING RUG! PERFECT FOR PARTIES!"

Then he performed a little tap dance on the rug.

"SQUAWK! SQUAWK! SQUAWK! SQUAWK! SQUAWK! SQUAWK! SQUAWK!"

As Cedric raised his head, no doubt about to peck Torrone's bottom, Butler grabbed the man's arm and tugged him away.

"You simply must see the chandelier! It's the pride of

Blunder Hall! This way."

Once inside the dining room, the most bizarre sight greeted them.

Suspended from the ceiling was Betsy, covered from head to toe in Christmas baubles!

CLINK! CLANK! CLUNK! went the chandelier as it swayed.

"Is that a foot poking out the bottom?" asked Torrone.

"Oh yes! So it is!" replied Butler, turning a deathly shade of pale.

"What is it doing there?"

"Erm, um…"

"WELL?" demanded Torrone as Butler squirmed.

"I told you it was a one-off, sir! You will never find another chandelier like it! Do you have chandeliers in America with feet sticking out of the bottom?"

"No."

"Then you will be the envy of all of New York society!"

Torrone's eyes lit up at the thought. "I'll take it! I'll take the lot! Boys! Give this fossil the dough!"

Butler smiled as the briefcase was opened, revealing

what must be a million dollars! A huge wad of hundred-dollar bills was handed to Butler. It was all the money the Blunders needed to save Blunder Hall. And to buy another tin of baked beans. Oh, and that hamster.

"Now load the lot into the plane."

Butler's face turned white with fear.

This was the fatal flaw in the plan that he'd been trying to put his finger on!

X

Blunder Hall would be saved, but there would be no Blunders in it! Instead, they would have to spend the rest of their lives standing very still in a gangster's apartment a hundred floors up in New York City!

Torrone marched out of the dining room into the hall, Butler trailing after him.

"But! But! But!" spluttered Butler.

"What now?" barked Torrone.

"Can't I post everything to you?"

Torrone looked at the old man as if he were bananas. "Post them?"

"Yes! I have plenty of stamps! I can post all the antiques off to you in America first thing tomorrow morning, if they fit into the postbox, of course."

Torrone smelled a rat. He took a huge puff on his cigar, then blew the thick cloud of smoke straight into Butler's face.

The old man coughed and spluttered.

"Nice try, wise guy!" snarled Torrone, before turning to his heavies. "Put everything in the plane! Now!"

Butler looked on in horror as each brute lifted an "antique", slung it over their shoulder and marched past.

"STOP!" he cried, but no one did.

As Cedric passed by, he snatched the money out of Butler's hand with his beak.

"SQUAWK!"

"Good work, Cedric!" hissed Bertie from inside the grandfather clock. "The man from the bank can have it first thing in the morning!"

"Wait..." called Butler.

But before he could say whatever he was going to say, the Blunders were gone.

The butler shuffled back into the dining room. He peered through the baked-bean-splattered window to see the Blunders being loaded into the plane.

"I'm so sorry, Blunders!" he muttered, a tear welling in his eye. "I'm going to miss you."

As the plane took off, he gently waved them goodbye.

Then, just as the plane was about to disappear into the clouds, one by one the "antiques" leaped out of the door.

"NO!" cried Butler.

But his fears were unfounded, as five parachutes opened!

WOOMPH!

The Blunders had escaped!

The family were not so silly after all!

As the five floated safely down to the ground, Butler shuffled out into the garden to greet them.

When they landed, the grandfather clock fell to pieces. Bertie was free.

The papier-mâché cracked, releasing Old Lady Blunder.

The Christmas baubles bounced off Betsy.

Brutus was released from the picture frame.

The tin foil unravelled, revealing Bunny.

"Thank goodness you found some parachutes!" exclaimed Butler. "But where is Cedric?"

All eyes swivelled to the sky.

"THERE HE IS!" shouted Brutus.

Cedric had no parachute. There is very little market making parachutes for birds. Even ostriches. He was desperately flapping his wings, but it wasn't making the least bit of difference.

The bird cried for help as he plummeted down, down, down.

"SQUAWK!"

As Cedric's mouth opened, he let go of the wad of hundred-dollar bills!

The bills fluttered off over the horizon, never to be seen again.

"NOOOO!" cried Bertie from the ground.
Now Cedric was falling at terrific speed.

WHOOSH!

"SQUAWK!"

The Blunders all ran around
the lawn to catch him, like
fielders in a cricket match.

However, this
was no cricket ball – this was
a full-sized ostrich!

Bertie sprinted and held
out his hands.

"I'VE GOT
HIM!" he
shouted.

Then, seeing
the big bird hurtle
towards him, he had
second thoughts.

"Oh dear!" he said as
Cedric crash-landed
on top of him.

Bertie was knocked out cold.

DONK!

He toppled forward and landed on the lawn with a

THOMP!

Cedric was unharmed. He fluttered his wings and sprang to his feet.

"SQUAWK!"

However, it seemed that this was the end for Bertie. The Blunders and Butler rushed over to him.

"LORD BLUNDER!"

"DARLING!"

"PAPAPAPAPAPAPAPA!"

"BERTRAM!"

"Don't tell me he's gone!" wailed Betsy.

Cedric's neck stretched down to Bertie. He nudged his head against his back, but there was no response.

"He's gone!" yowled Bunny. "PAPAPAPAPAPA PAPAPAPAPAPAPAPA!"

Then Cedric had a better idea. He pecked Bertie's bottom. PECK!

"OOOWWWEEE!" cried Bertie.

He was alive!

Bertie scrambled to his feet, clutching his behind. PECK! PECK! PECK!

"Well done, darling! You saved Cedric!" said Betsy, hugging him.

"Did I?"

"Well, sort of! How do you feel?"

"With my hands, normally."

"No, how do you feel inside?" she asked.

"That is much harder."

"Do you need anything?"

"Rather!" murmured the others.

"I am sorry to say, Blunders, that we don't have any tea in the house," replied Butler. "I could try to make some baked-bean-flavoured tea."

"How?" asked Bertie.

"With all the baked-bean juice still splattered over the windows."

"SOUNDS SCRUMPTIOUS!" said Bertie as the Blunders skipped back into the house together.

A
DEADLY GAME
OF
SNAKES AND LADDERS

A dramatic storm had descended on Blunder Hall.

THUNDER ROLLED.

LIGHTNING STRUCK.

RAIN LASHED.

The storm was so brutal that the Blunders were trapped inside the house.

Butler had been given the task of catching all the rainwater that was streaming through the roof. He had placed a maze of buckets, pans and bowls all over the floor.

PLINK! PLONK! **PLUNK!** went the drips.

The Blunders had to skip, hop and jump over them.

Not being able to go outside, the children had spent the whole day inside playing pranks on each other.

Brutus hid a huge cockroach down the toilet. So, when Bunny sat on the toilet seat, her bottom got a nasty surprise.

SNAP!

"YEOW!"

In revenge, Bunny took all the stuffing out of the sofa so, when Brutus slumped down on to it, it swallowed him whole.

"GUH!"

Brutus spread his huge collection of marbles over Bunny's bedroom floor. So, when she stepped inside, she rolled all over the room, crashing into everything!

DONK! DONK! DONK!

Next, Bunny hid an ants' nest in Brutus's chest of drawers. Now the boy had ants in his pants. His bottom itched like crazy.

"OH! UH! AH!"

Brutus sawed a trapdoor in the floor outside Bunny's bedroom. Then he placed a rug on top of it. As soon as she stepped on it, she fell through the floor…

W H O O S H!

"ARGH!"

…landing on the armchair in the library below.

BOING!

Bunny poured a pot of honey into Brutus's boots.

136

His feet became stuck inside.

"URGH!" he cried as he tried in vain to prise his boots off.

SQUELCH!

Their mother had a not-so-bright idea. She called the children into the living room, where Old Lady Blunder was snoozing in an armchair, clutching her blunderbuss.

"Bunny! Brutus!" began Betsy. "I've just had the most awfully clever thought!"

"Mamamamama, that doesn't sound like you," replied Bunny. "Do you need to have a lie down?"

"Actually, I tell a fib! It was Pegasus's idea."

"Here we go!" sighed Brutus.

"Why don't you two play a nice game of Snakes and Ladders?"

"Because we would rather torment each other!" replied Bunny.

"And because Snakes and Ladders is BORING!" added Brutus.

"You are BORING!"

"No! You are the BORING one, Bunny!"

"BORING! BORING! BORING!" she chanted.

"BORING! BORING! BORING!" he chanted back.

"Please!" pleaded their mother.

"BORING! BORING! BORING!" they chanted together.

"IF YOU DON'T BOTH PUT A SOCK IN IT," said Betsy, "THERE WILL BE NO MORE HOMEWORK!"

"HURRAH!" cried the kids.

This threat had backfired.

From her armchair, Old Lady Blunder opened one eye.

"WHAT'S ALL THIS HULLABALOO?" she thundered.

"I just want the children to behave, and play a lovely game of Snakes and Ladders," replied Betsy.

"BORING! BORING! BORING!" chanted Bunny and Brutus.

Old Lady Blunder raised her blunderbuss and fired it at the ceiling.

BANG!

The children fell silent as dust and debris descended on to them.

"Actually," began Bunny, "I would love to play Snakes and Ladders!"

"Me too!" agreed Brutus.

"You see, Betsy dear," said Old Lady Blunder. "All children need is a little gentle persuasion."

Betsy asked Butler to go up to the loft to fetch the Snakes and Ladders box.

Carrying a long ladder, he wound his way up the hundreds of stairs in Blunder Hall.

Once he'd reached the top, he positioned the ladder with great care so it wouldn't fall. Then he shuffled up it as fast as a sloth.

When he reached the hatch, he looked down and realised how high he was. He was dizzy with vertigo.

"Onwards and upwards," he muttered to himself.

The loft stretched all the way under the leaking roof of Blunder Hall. No one had been up here for years.

"I wonder if there is any treasure," said Butler to himself. "Something that might pay off this most unfortunate debt."

Sadly, the loft was a treasure trove of junk.

Butler was disappointed to find:

- A thousand-piece jigsaw with just one piece.

- Boxes and boxes of unsold uni-shoes.
- A carriage clock with no hands.
- An old tin bath that had rusted so much it had hundreds of holes.

- An ostrich egg cup.
- A dining chair with just two legs.
- Books that had become so wet from the rainwater that all the words had been washed off the pages. Ideal for non-readers.
- A handle with no cup.
- A stuffed ant.
- A train set with no train. And no track.

Nothing you could give away, let alone sell.

"Oh dear," muttered Butler to himself. "Not a sausage to save Blunder Hall here. Now, where is this Snakes and Ladders set?"

Eventually, after searching under a sack of odd socks, he found the game.

"MISSION ACCOMPLISHED!" he exclaimed.

Flushed with success, he hurried back to the hatch.

Butler put his foot out to step on the ladder but…

…IT WASN'T THERE!

He stumbled.

"ARGH!"

He dropped through the hatch!

WHOOSH!

Butler reached out his hand just in time! He found himself clinging to the edge of the hatch by his forefinger!

It was an awfully long way down. If he fell, he would break every bone in his body.

"HELP!" he cried as he dangled there. "HELP!"

Fortunately, Butler heard footsteps coming up the stairs.

"HELP!" he cried again, louder this time.

"SQUAWK!"

It was the Blunders' pet ostrich!

"Cedric!" exclaimed Butler.

"Thank goodness you are here!"

"SQUAWK!"

"Cedric, please would you be so kind as to peck Lord Blunder on the bottom and bring him up here at once?"

The bird tilted his head, trying to understand.

"SQUAWK!"

"I know!" exclaimed Butler, launching into a mime. He performed an impression of the ostrich pecking, and then an impression of Bertie having his bottom pecked.

Cedric eagerly nodded his head and raced back down the stairs.

"SQUAWK!"

In no time, there was the sound of pecking and someone shouting "ouch".

PECK! PECK! PECK!

"OUCH! OUCH! OUCH!"

Cedric kept on pecking until Bertie was standing right under the dangling Butler. Then he stopped and bounded off.

"BLASTED BIRD!" exclaimed Bertie.

Butler called down, "Excuse me, your lordship!"

Bertie looked every which way but up. "Where the devil are you?"

"Up here, sir."

Bertie looked down.

"Other up, sir!"

Bertie looked up.

"Butler! What the blazes are you doing all the way up there?"

"I was retrieving the Snakes and Ladders set for young Miss Bunny and young Master Brutus."

"Jolly good show!"

With that Bertie strode off along the corridor.

"Sir?"

"Yes, Butler?"

"Have you seen a ladder?"

"No."

"Are you sure?"

"What does this ladder look like?"

"Laddery?"

"No! No! No! No! Not seen it. Oh no! Oh, yes! Yes! Yes!

I have seen a long wooden blighter with rungs."

"That's it, your lordship. Do you know where this ladder went?"

"Yes, I do," replied Bertie, waltzing off.

"Please could you tell me where it is, sir?" cried Butler.

"On the fire."

"On the fire?"

"On the fire."

"Why is the ladder on the fire?"

"Blasted cold in this house on account of this rotten weather! So I chopped it up and hurled it on the fire."

"Why didn't you use the firewood?"

"I was saving that in case of an emergency!"

"What emergency? This is an emergency! How am I going to get down?"

"I am sorry, Butler. We can't splash out on another ladder right now, because of all this blasted money we owe this blasted man from the bank. I could pop into the village on Monday and see if the man from the bank might lend me some more money to buy a new ladder. But I am not sure it would go down well."

"If I lose my grip, sir, I'm not going to go down well!"

"Can it wait until Monday?"

"No!"

"Then let me give your predicament some serious thought."

There was a long pause.

"Please don't take too much time to think, sir. I'm not sure I can hold on for much longer!"

"Hmm," said Bertie. It was a sound he'd heard people make when they were thinking. "Oh, my giddy aunt! I've got it!"

"Yes, sir?"

"I can see the Snakes and Ladders box under your arm. Why can't you use one of those ladders?"

Butler sighed. "With all due respect, your lordship, that is not going to work."

"Oh yes! Silly me! You go up the ladders! You can only slide down the snakes!"

"That is still not going to work, sir!"

"I'VE GOT IT! I'M A GENIUS! SIMPLY TURN THE SNAKES AND LADDERS BOARD UPSIDE DOWN!"

Butler shook his head. This was SILLINESS on an EPIC scale!

"Sir, perhaps you could get all the Blunders together to see if anyone can think of a plan?"

"Splendid! I will gather the troops, Butler! Hang on!"

"The thought had occurred to me."

As Bertie disappeared in one direction, his mother appeared in another.

"Your ladyship!"

"WHO GOES THERE?" she barked, raising her blunderbuss.

"It's me – Butler. I was wondering…"

"SPIT IT OUT, MAN, FOR GOODNESS' SAKE!"

"I was wondering if you could please help me get down?"

Old Lady Blunder looked up and down a few times, before a thought flashed across her eyes.

"I could always shoot you down!" she said.

"That's very kind of you, ma'am, but no."

"Why ever not?"

"Because I'd be dead."

"Do you want to get down or not?"

"Yes, but preferably alive."

"Spoilsport!" she huffed, stomping off down the

corridor. "I'm off to bed!"

"That's it!" said Butler to himself. "All I need is a sheet!"

After what felt like an age, Bertie returned, alone.

"Hello again!" he chirped.

"Forgive me, sir, but where are the rest of the Blunders?"

"Mother went to bed."

"Yes, I saw."

"She needs her beauty sleep."

"Yes, I saw."

"Sorry to say, but the rest of the Blunders are rather busy."

"May I ask, doing what?"

"Well, Bunny and Brutus are busy waiting for you to bring down the Snakes and Ladders set."

"Of course! And Lady Blunder?"

"She is busy cantering round and round the ballroom riding her imaginary horse."

"You have to have a hobby… Now, please could you find the biggest sheet in Blunder Hall and bring it here!"

"Of course, my man! Over and out!"

*

After another age, Bertie returned holding a sheet.

Of paper.

"This is the biggest sheet I could find!" he said, proudly holding it up.

"I meant a bedsheet, your lordship!"

"Hmm. You really should have made that clear. I did think it was peculiar that you wanted to write a letter while you were dangling from the loft."

"Lord Blunder, please could you return with the biggest bedsheet you can find, and your wife and children? I am not sure I can hold on much longer. This is a matter of life and death!"

After yet another age, Bertie and his fellow Blunders stomped up flight after flight of stairs to reach the top of Blunder Hall. And, miracle of miracles, Bertie was holding a bedsheet. A moth-eaten one, but still a bedsheet.

"Thank you! Thank you! Thank you!" exclaimed Butler. "Now, if everyone holds a corner of the sheet tight, then I can let go and you can break my fall!"

"PERFECT!" replied Bertie.

The Blunders held the four corners of the sheet tight

and shuffled into place.

"EXCELLENT!" said Butler. "Now I will drop down in three, two, one!"

On one, Butler shut his eyes tight and let go.

WHOOSH!

"GERONIMO!"

He landed in the dead centre of the sheet!

BOING!

The Butlers all yanked on their corner to break Butler's fall, but in doing so…

WHOOSH!

...they sent him right back up to where he'd come from.

Butler grabbed hold of the loft hatch again.

"Bother!" he said.

Then he heard a voice from below. It was Betsy.

"Butler?"

"Yes, ma'am?"

"As it appears that you will be dangling there forever, would you be kind enough to drop the Snakes and Ladders set down?"

Ever the dutiful butler, Butler did as he was asked. "Of course, ma'am. Ready?"

"Ready!" replied Betsy.

Butler gently dropped the box from under his arm. Betsy fumbled, failing to catch it. Instead, it hit her head.

DOINK!

"OUCH!"

The box broke, the board snapped in half and all the counters and dice scattered.

"OOPS!" she added.

"Well, that's that, Butler," said Bertie. "We will hurl a cup of tea and a biscuit to you now and again. We will miss you, but we wish you all the best for the future."

He took his wife's hand and headed off down the stairs.

"You can't just leave me dangling!"

"No?"

"NO!"

"Butler?" said Bertie.

"Yes, sir?"

"Would you mind awfully popping down and clearing up this mess?"

"I can't, sir. If I let go, I will only create more mess."

"I've got it!" exclaimed Brutus. "It's so simple it's brilliant!"

"Do tell us," replied Bunny.

"It's been staring us all in the face!"

"What has?"

"The answer!"

"What is it, then?" demanded Bunny.

"Just like in the game, Butler went up the ladder. So, why doesn't he slide down a snake?"

"Because we don't have a snake!"

"No, but I know where to find one!" declared Brutus. "Follow me!"

Brutus was the Blunder who was most in touch with nature. By which I mean he often had a toad in his pocket, a jar full to the brim with live maggots or a slug stuck up his nose, as this handy diagram shows.

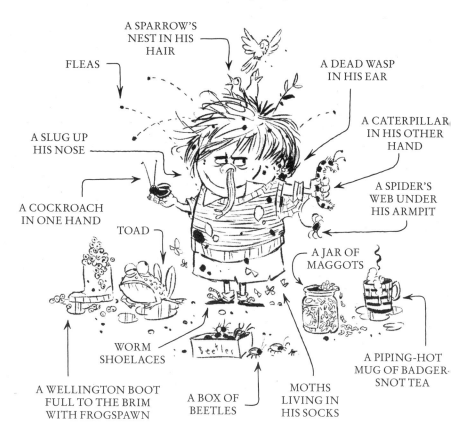

A SPARROW'S NEST IN HIS HAIR

FLEAS

A DEAD WASP IN HIS EAR

A CATERPILLAR IN HIS OTHER HAND

A SLUG UP HIS NOSE

A SPIDER'S WEB UNDER HIS ARMPIT

A COCKROACH IN ONE HAND

TOAD

A JAR OF MAGGOTS

WORM SHOELACES

A WELLINGTON BOOT FULL TO THE BRIM WITH FROGSPAWN

A BOX OF BEETLES

MOTHS LIVING IN HIS SOCKS

A PIPING-HOT MUG OF BADGER SNOT TEA

Old Lady Blunder was woken from her slumber, and all the Blunders assembled in the hall.

"LET ME HUNT THIS GIANT SNAKE ALONE!" said Old Lady Blunder. She was still in her nightdress, clutching her blunderbuss.

"It's too dangerous, Grandmamamamama!" said Bunny.

"When I was your age, I hunted pythons in Belgium!"

"Belgium?" asked Brutus. "Are there any pythons in Belgium?"

"No. Which made them devilishly difficult to hunt."

"Are there any snakes in England?" asked Betsy.

"Not many," replied Brutus, "but there are lots and lots of worms."

"WORMS?" thundered Old Lady Blunder.

"They're the next best thing to snakes!" declared Brutus.

"Hardly! It's not called Worms and Ladders!"

"How can Butler slide down a worm?" scoffed Bunny.

"If we find a long enough worm, it might just work!" replied Brutus. "I have caught some whoppers over the years! We just need to dig up the garden and find one!"

"There is a storm raging outside!" exclaimed Bunny.

"And it's gone midnight!" added Betsy.

"The perfect time to find worms! They love the rain, and they love the dark. Follow me!"

Soon the Blunders were out in the garden, soaked to the skin and shivering with cold.

There was just the one spade, which Old Lady Blunder had commandeered to dig up the lawn.

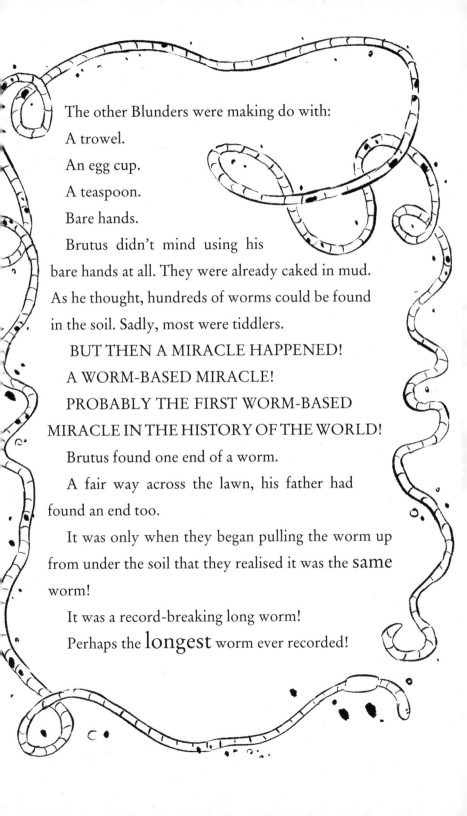

The other Blunders were making do with:

A trowel.

An egg cup.

A teaspoon.

Bare hands.

Brutus didn't mind using his bare hands at all. They were already caked in mud. As he thought, hundreds of worms could be found in the soil. Sadly, most were tiddlers.

BUT THEN A MIRACLE HAPPENED!

A WORM-BASED MIRACLE!

PROBABLY THE FIRST WORM-BASED MIRACLE IN THE HISTORY OF THE WORLD!

Brutus found one end of a worm.

A fair way across the lawn, his father had found an end too.

It was only when they began pulling the worm up from under the soil that they realised it was the same worm!

It was a record-breaking long worm!

Perhaps the longest worm ever recorded!

On seeing this impossibly long worm, Old Lady Blunder reached for her blunderbuss.

"STAND BACK!" she shouted. "I am going to blast this brute all the way to BELGIUM!"

"NO!" cried Brutus, positioning himself between the blunderbuss and the worm. "This worm is my friend. I call him Shorty, and he needs to live! Shorty is our only hope if Butler is going to be able to slide down from the loft!"

"But how can you slide down a worm?" asked Bunny.

"Gently?" guessed her mother.

Within moments, the soggy Blunders were back in Blunder Hall. They marched up the stairs to tell Butler the good news.

"A WORM?" he exclaimed.

"Yes. A worm is the closest thing we could find to a snake," replied Bertie. "Which got me thinking... I could invent a game called Worms and Snakes! That would make billions!"

"No, it wouldn't, Bertram," said his mother. "Do shut up, there's a good boy!"

"With respect," said Butler, "I'm not going to be able to slide down a w—"

"That's settled, then," said Brutus. "I will throw up one end of Shorty! You just need to catch him. Here we go. One! Two! Three!"

The boy swung the worm up to the hatch.

Butler reached out to catch hold of the worm, but, before he could, Cedric the ostrich hopped down the hall.

"SQUAWK!"

He seized the end of Shorty in his beak and bounded off with him. No doubt to gobble him up!

What Cedric hadn't reckoned with, and we can forgive him, as he is an ostrich, was that Brutus was still holding on to the other end of the worm.

The worm went... T W O N G !

"HELP!" cried Brutus.

The Blunders gathered round him and grasped the end.

Like a tug of war, they heaved and heaved and heaved, but Cedric wouldn't let go.

"TICKLE HIM!" shouted Butler from the hatch.

"WHO?" asked Bertie. "ME?"

"NO! CEDRIC!"

Bertie stepped forward with trepidation. He reached out his hand and tickled the ostrich under his chin.

"SQUAWK!"

The bird's beak opened, and the end of the worm snapped out.

It bounced back and hit Bunny in the eye.

"EURGH!" she cried.

Cedric was not giving up. HE WANTED THAT WORM! The bird made a daring leap at the Blunders, knocking them to the floor.

"OOF!"

The Blunders found themselves being trampled by their pet ostrich. They needed a plan! AND FAST!

"TICKLE HIM AGAIN, PAPAPAPAPA!" shouted Bunny.

Unfortunately for Bertie, but fortunately for his fellow Blunders, his head was just underneath the ostrich's behind.

He shut his eyes tight and reached out his hand.

Now, no one likes their bottom tickled at the best of times.

CEDRIC HATED IT!

"SQUAWK!" he squawked, leaping up into the air.

WHOOSH!

The ostrich leaped so high that he bashed into Butler.

BOSH!

Butler lost his grip and fell on to the bird's back.

DOOF!

"SQUAWK!"

If he'd thought that Cedric
was going to fly safely
down to the floor,
he was wrong.
Ostriches can't fly!
Instead, the pair fell
through the air and
landed right on
top of the Blunders!

BOOSH!

Butler and Cedric were unharmed, but the Blunders lay in a dazed heap on the floor. Butler grabbed the worm and stuffed it in his breast pocket. With Cedric in pursuit, Butler leaped on the bannister and slid down to the bottom on his bottom.

WHIZZ!

The ostrich sprang down the stairs after him!

"SQUAWK!"

Butler shuffled over to the back door as fast as he could shuffle. He made it just in time, slamming the door shut on Cedric.

"SQUAWK! SQUAWK! SQUAWK!" squawked Cedric, pecking his beak on the window.

PLINK! PLINK! PLINK!

He wanted that worm more than anything in the world.

Butler threw a smug look back at the bird as he shuffled across the lawn.

The storm had passed, and now it was dawn. The sun was rising behind the trees. Butler placed the worm on the ground, and watched as it burrowed its way back under the earth.

"There you go, Shorty," he said, beaming with pride at a good deed done.

Just as he began to lumber off, a now all-too-familiar figure strode on to the lawn.

IT WAS THE MAN FROM THE BANK!

Trailing behind the man from the bank marched an army of builders!

"Can I help you, sirs?" asked Butler.

"NO! YOU CANNOT!" the man from the bank barked back.

"May I ask what you are doing on the Blunder family lawn?"

"These are the builders who, in a few weeks' time, will be transforming Blunder Hall into Blunder Borstal!" The man from the bank took a large paper plan out of his briefcase. At the top was written

BLUNDER BORSTAL.

It detailed all the changes that he was poised to make to Blunder Hall.

As the man from the bank consulted his plan, he turned to the builders. "This wing is where the extremely naughty children will be put, so we need all these windows to be bricked up..."

The Blunders were outraged at this uninvited guest. They stormed out of their house, and over to the man.

"HOW DARE YOU COME UNINVITED ON TO OUR LAWN?" thundered Old Lady Blunder.

"I do dare, madam! I do! Because, before long, Blunder Hall, and everything in it, will belong to the bank! I would start packing your bags now, Blunders!"

"You heartless brute!" said Betsy.

"Oh, Mamamamamama, don't cry," said Bunny, putting her arm round her mother.

"Where is Shorty when you need him?" asked Brutus. "SHORTY!"

"Who is Shorty?" said the man from the bank.

"Oh! With any luck, you'll meet him! SHORTY!"

What was lucky for the Blunders was unlucky for the man from the bank.

One end of the world's longest worm poked out of the lawn. It wrapped itself round the man's ankle.

"ARGH!" he cried as the worm dragged him down under the ground.

The builders tried to grab him, but Shorty was too quick.

THRUMBLE!

In moments, there was no sign of Shorty or the man from the bank. All that was left was a large mound of earth on the lawn.

"I suppose we should rescue him," said Bertie.

"Let's not be too hasty!" replied Old Lady Blunder. "It's teatime!"

With that, she turned and marched off, leading the family back into their home.

Unfortunately for them, the builders dug down and hoisted out the man from the bank. He was covered in soil and looked more like a mole than ever. And he had already looked a lot like a mole.

"BLUNDERS!" he bellowed, spitting soil from his mouth as he spoke. His tongue was black. "I WILL BE BACK! BACK TO SEIZE BLUNDER HALL FROM YOU BLUNDERSOME BUFFOONS!"

THE
SCANDAL
OF THE
GIANT MARROW

"WE WILL WIN FIRST PRIZE! IT IS A MATTER OF FAMILY PRIDE! WE BLUNDERS WILL BE VICTORIOUS!"

Bertie Blunder was expounding on the village marrow-growing competition. A competition in which he had come last for the past few decades. His tiny marrows had failed to impress. Some had even been disqualified altogether for being too small.

This year, with Blunder Hall under threat, Bertie was more determined to win than ever.

"This blasted business with the bank has taken its toll on all of us," he said as he looked round the living room at the faces of his family. "Winning the village marrow-growing competition would be the boost we Blunders need!"

"What do we win?" asked Bunny.

"A giant jar of marmalade!"

"How is a giant jar of marmalade going to help us save Blunder Hall?" asked Brutus.

"It's a symbol, boy!" replied Old Lady Blunder. "A symbol that we Blunders mean business!"

"Or, if the jar is big enough," began Betsy, "perhaps we can trap the man from the bank inside it? Like a wasp."

"It's not that big, dear," said Bertie. "But I tell you what *is* BIG! BIGGER THAN BIG! BIGNORMOUS!"

"WHAT?" demanded Old Lady Blunder.

"MY MARROW! To the greenhouse! Follow me!"

The Blunders trailed out of Blunder Hall after Bertie.

"WHOA, PEGASUS!" said Betsy to her imaginary horse as she cantered across the grass.

Cedric, who had been pecking at the ground in search of worms, popped his head up and followed the family.

"SQUAWK!"

For a moment, the house and garden were cast into

a huge shadow. The Blunders looked up.

An airship was passing directly overhead.

"LOOK!" shouted Brutus, pointing at it.

"Never seen one of those flying over Blunder Hall before," said Old Lady Blunder, stopping. "What is it doing up there?"

"It's flying, Mother," replied Bertie. "Now, please, everyone, keep up. You don't want to miss the grand unveiling!"

He strode ahead before opening the door to the battered old greenhouse, the handle coming off in his hand.

"Oops!" he said.

Cobwebs lurked in every corner.

There was an infestation of greenfly.

Mould crept up the walls.

And it ponged.

"BEHOLD!" exclaimed Bertie as he whipped a sheet off a bag of soil. "MY MIGHTY MARROW!"

His fellow Blunders leaned over to see the tiniest, wrinkliest, shriveliest marrow in the known universe.

"Darling? Are you sure that isn't a baby courgette?" asked Betsy.

"Only one way to find out!" said Old Lady Blunder, raising her blunderbuss. "BLAST THE BLIGHTER TO SMITHEREENS!"

"NO! NO! NO! MOTHER!" pleaded Bertie. "It might still grow! Show my marrow mercy!"

Brutus snorted. "It would be merciful to flush that thing straight down the toilet!"

"It would be merciful to flush *you* down the toilet!" said Bunny.

"I've already tried to flush myself down the toilet and I didn't fit!"

"I would have gladly poked you down with a brush!"

"Children, please," said Betsy. "You are upsetting Pegasus. WHOA, THERE!"

"I'm so sorry, Papapapa, but you could only win a smallest-marrow competition with this," said Bunny.

"But I used magic manure!"

"What's in your magic manure? Don't tell me it's your doobries!"

"No! Ostrich doobries!"

"SQUAWK!" agreed Cedric.

"You should have asked Pegasus for *his* doobries!" said Betsy. "He would have been only too happy to oblige, wouldn't you, Pegasus? Oh! He's doing a doobry for you now! Oh! That's a mighty one! Good boy!"

She looked down at a big mound of nothing on the floor.

With Bertie distracted, Cedric came up behind him and pecked the marrow out of the soil.

"SQUAWK!"

The ostrich gobbled the morsel down in one.

"I have let you Blunders down again," said Bertie sorrowfully. "I am so, so sorry."

Old Lady Blunder placed her hand on her son's shoulder and squeezed hard. As she spoke, Bertie whined at the pain.

"You know, boy, there is an old Blunder saying, passed down through generations of Blunders, a sacred code that has served us Blunders for centuries!"

"What is it, Mamamamama?"

"IF IN DOUBT, CHEAT!"

II

The airship was now circling over Blunder Hall, a sinister symbol revealed on its side.

"A SWASTIKA!" exclaimed Brutus.

"NAZIS!" agreed Old Lady Blunder. "BUT WE ARE NOT AT WAR! WELL, NOT YET!"

"This could be a surprise attack!" guessed Brutus.

The boy guessed right. At that moment, there was the howl of gunfire.

RAT-TAT-TAT!

The airship was armed with machine guns!

RAT-TAT-TAT!

The greenhouse was shot to smithereens.

RAT-TAT-TAT!

"GET DOWN!" shouted Bertie, shielding his wife and children under him.

Betsy's bottom was buzzing with nerves, and she let out a raspberry.

PFFFT!

"Naughty Pegasus!" she lied.

"MAMAMAMAMA! GET DOWN!" pleaded Bertie.

"NEVER!" replied Old Lady Blunder, standing her ground. As the grass around her was torn to shreds by bullets, she calmly raised her blunderbuss and fired.

BANG!

"BINGO!" she cried. The airship was hit.

Like a party balloon that had been blown up but not tied, the airship whizzed all over the sky.

W H O O S H !

It made a rude noise as it flew.

SPLURT!

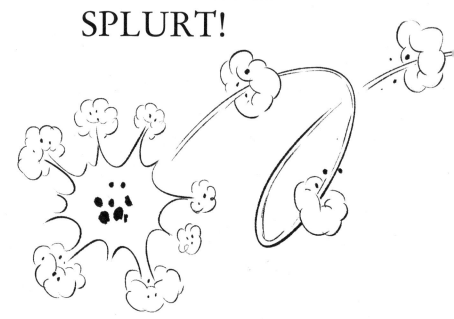

As it performed a loop
the loop, the pilot leaped out.

WOOMPH!

His parachute opened as the airless envelope (the balloon bit) whizzed down to the ground.

WHOOSH!

It landed right on top of Bertie.

"HELP!" he cried.

"WHO SAID THAT?" demanded Old Lady Blunder.

"Me!"

"ME WHO?"

"Bertie!"

"BERTIE WHO?"

"Your son!"

"Oh yes! Why didn't you say so? Where are you?"

"Trapped under the airship!"

"Stay there! We are coming in!"

As the Blunders dragged Bertie out by his feet, Old Lady Blunder looked up at the sky. There was no parachute to be seen.

"Did anyone see where the pilot landed?" asked Old Lady Blunder.

"No!" replied the others.

"Perhaps he plunged into the village pond and is being nibbled to death by tadpoles!" said Brutus.

"We can but pray!" replied Bertie. "Well, what a lucky turn of events!"

"LUCKY?" spluttered Bunny. "We were nearly all

blasted to bits!"

"*That* was unlucky, I will grant you that! But, my fellow Blunders, we are now looking at our prize-winning marrow!"

He gestured towards the crumpled balloon.

"Papapapapa!" exclaimed Bunny. "You don't mean...?"

"I do mean! This could be my greatest invention yet – an airship marrow!"

"A *what* what?"

"BLUNDERS! WE ARE GOING TO TRANSFORM THIS AIRSHIP INTO A GIANT MARROW!"

I don't know if you have ever tried transforming an airship into a giant marrow, but it is not an easy task.

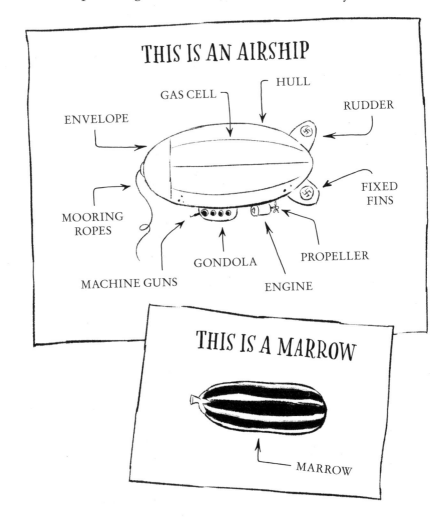

THIS IS AN AIRSHIP

HULL

GAS CELL

ENVELOPE

RUDDER

FIXED
FINS

MOORING
ROPES

MACHINE GUNS

GONDOLA

ENGINE

PROPELLER

THIS IS A MARROW

MARROW

"If we Blunders pull this off, people will come from all over the world to marvel at our marrow!" exclaimed Bertie. "We could make a fortune! Then, when every last person in the world has seen it, we could make an ocean of marrow soup!"

"But, Papapapapa, it will be made of air, not marrow," replied Bunny.

"All right, then, AIR SOUP! BLUNDERS, ASSEMBLE! Here are your tasks!"

As soon as Bertie had their attention, he began.

"Cedric! Use your beak and this piece of thread to sew up the hole my mamamamama's blunderbuss made!"

It was quite a delicate task to give to an ostrich, but Cedric squawked "yes"...

"SQUAWK!"

...and tried his best to sew with his beak.

"Brutus! Your task is to paint this airship marrow green!"

"What do I get?"

"You get a pot of green paint!"

He handed his son a pot and a brush, and reluctantly the boy went to work.

"NOT FAIR, PAPAPAPAPA!" cried Bunny, stamping her feet. "I WANTED TO DO THE PAINTING!"

"You still can! That's the beauty of the scheme! Bunny, you must paint yellow stripes on the airship to make it look like a marrow!"

"I HATE YELLOW!"

Old Lady Blunder stepped in. "Bertram, please let me handle this! NOW GET ON WITH IT, CHILD! OR I WILL BE FORCED TO HOLD YOU UPSIDE DOWN, AND DUNK YOUR HEAD IN THIS POT OF PAINT!"

Without another word, Bunny began.

"BETSY!" cried Bertie.

"Oh, darling! I feel so ashamed about what happened earlier!" she replied.

"Please, my love, don't worry. We all know your bottom has a mind of its own! Now I need you to pedal the Baroness from the front of Blunder Hall round to the back."

"Righto!" she replied. "Pegasus! RUN LIKE THE WIND! NOT MY WIND! I MEAN THE OTHER WIND!"

"BUTLER!" called Bertie.

Butler the butler shuffled out of the house, and across the lawn.

"Yes, your lordship?"

"You are a strapping young man of ninety-nine, so I have assigned you the **mightiest** task of all."

"Yes?"

"YOU ARE TO BLOW UP THE BALLOON!"

"I am sorry, sir. I don't think I quite heard you right. You want me to blow up the balloon?"

"YES!"

"But we don't have a pump!"

"You don't need a pump! ALL YOU NEED IS A BIT OF HUFF AND PUFF!"

Butler shuffled over to the balloon. He pinched the end, took a deep breath and blew.

FOOF!

Finally, Bertie approached his mother.

"Mamamamama?"

"Yes, Bertram?"

"Your job is not to shoot anything."

"I can't make any promises, but I will do my best!"

BANG!

*

Things got off to a shaky start.

Brutus painted Bunny green.

"HA! HA!"

In revenge, Bunny painted Brutus yellow.

"HEE! HEE!"

Betsy pedalled the Rolls-Royce straight into a tree.

KERUNCH!

However, by dawn, Butler had huffed and puffed so much that the balloon began to bounce off the ground.

BOING! BOING! BOING!

"YOU DID IT!" exclaimed Bertie. "BUTLER! YOU DID IT!"

Bounding over to embrace the man, Bertie
stepped into a pot of green paint. His foot got stuck.

PLONK!

Then he stepped into a pot of yellow paint.

PLONK!

With paint pots for shoes,
Bertie took a tumble –
right into the balloon!

"OOF!"

The air shot out of the end so fast that it blew Butler off his feet!

P F F F T !

The poor man landed in a hedge.

RUSTLE!

As the balloon zoomed forward, it knocked over everyone and everything in sight.

Butler went back to work. By lunchtime, he had inflated the balloon once more, and carefully tied the end of it. He didn't want to have to blow it up all over again.

Painted green with yellow stripes, the airship was now THE MOST MARVELLOUS MARROW THE WORLD HAD EVER SEEN!

The question was, would anyone be fooled?

The most important person to fool was the vicar. He looked like a remarkably handsome pig.

SPOT THE DIFFERENCE

Every year for the past fifty years, the vicar had judged the village marrow-growing competition. As he rode through the gates of Blunder Hall on his tricycle, the family hid the giant marrow behind some tall trees at the end of the garden. It deserved to make a BIG ENTRANCE!

Next to arrive was an assortment of old ladies. Much like chocolates, they were all wrapped up in something colourful.

Butler was tasked with greeting everybody, and soon all the stalls for the village fete had been set up.

VILLAGE FETE

HOOK-A-DUCK
GUESS THE WEIGHT OF THE FRUIT CAKE
TOMBOLA
BRIC-A-BRAC
COCONUT SHY
FACE PAINTING
HOOPLA
CANDYFLOSS MACHINE
PIN THE TAIL ON THE DONKEY
WHITE ELEPHANT

The local farmer, Farmer Farmer, was a brute of a man, with a strong whiff of dung.

FARMER FARMER

PONG OF DOOBRIES (NOT HIS OWN)

FLAT CAP

SQUASHED NOSE (FROM BARE-KNUCKLE BOXING)

RUDDY FACE

STRAGGLY BEARD

CAULIFLOWER EAR (ALSO FROM BARE-KNUCKLE BOXING)

FISTS THE SIZE OF PUMPKINS

HOB-NAILED BOOTS

HOLES IN HIS TROUSERS CAUSED BY FERRET BITES

He set up a huge trestle table in the centre of the lawn, on to which all the keen gardeners placed their marrows. All impressive, but none a clear winner.

Then Farmer Farmer trundled his marrow towards the table on a wheelbarrow. He used all his brawn to lift it out. He thumped it down on the table.

DOOF!

All the other marrows flew up into the air.

"Mr Vicar, she's a beauty, ain't she? You might as well give me that giant jar of marmalade now!"

But before the vicar could reply, the Blunders emerged from behind the trees, pedalling their car.

And what did they have strapped to the roof?

A MASSIVE MARROW, OF COURSE!

The villagers stood open-mouthed in shock.

"WHAT THE...?" began Farmer Farmer.

But before he could say whatever rude word he was about to say, the Baroness bumped into the table.

THUMP!

Bertie Blunder opened a door of the Rolls-Royce. It fell off its hinges on to the lawn.

CLOMP!

Doing his best to ignore that, he chirped, "Good afternoon! And a huge welcome to Blunder Hall!"

The rest of the family climbed out of the Rolls and began untying the marrow from the roof.

"CAREFUL!" cried Bertie. "IT'S HEAVY!"

This was a ruse!

This massive marrow wasn't heavy at all – it was full of air, not marrowy stuff! The ropes were to stop it from floating away!

Bertie and Betsy Blunder held on to an end each as they guided the marrow over to the table. It bounced on to it, bouncing off all the other marrows.

PLOP! PLOP! PLOP!

Bertie accidentally put his foot through Farmer Farmer's marrow.

S Q U E L C H !

It was as if he had one marrow shoe.

SPOT THE DIFFERENCE

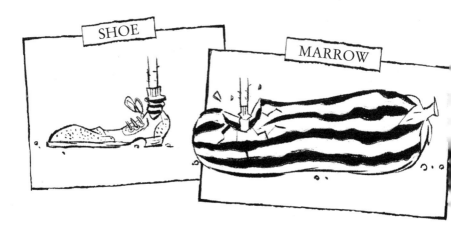

"NOOOOO!" snarled Farmer.

"I seem to have put my foot in it!" joked Bertie.

But the big man did not see the funny side. He grimaced and punched the palm of his hand.

BOF!

The vicar inspected this monstrosity with suspicion.

"Blunders! This is **not** a real marrow!" he declared.

"Vicar! Why ever would you say that?" asked Bertie, touching his nose to check it wasn't growing at the lie.

"Because," replied the vicar, "it is impossible for a marrow to grow to such gargantuan proportions!"

"HE USED MAGIC MANURE!" cried Betsy. "OSTRICH DOOBRIES!"

"I grew mine with hippopotamus doobries from the zoo," said Farmer Farmer, "and yet your marrow is a thousand times the size! How do you explain that?"

"My doobries are better than your doobries?" suggested Bertie.

Farmer loomed over Bertie menacingly. "HOW DARE YOU INSULT MY DOOBRIES!"

"Well, er, um," spluttered Bertie.

Fortunately, his mother stepped in to protect him. "FARMER FARMER! YOU ARE NOT TOO OLD FOR ME TO PUT YOU OVER MY KNEE!"

"I AM FIFTY-TWO!"

"EXACTLY!" she exclaimed, spitting on her hand, readying it to strike.

"PLEASE! PLEASE! PLEASE!" pleaded the vicar. "I have not come here today to referee a fight!"

"NO!" replied Brutus. "But could you?"

"Vicar! You came here to award us Blunders first prize for our massive marrow!" said Bunny.

"We will see about that, young lady!" said the vicar, narrowing his eyes until they were invisible. "I will need to give this so-called 'marrow' a taste check. Only that can confirm the marrow's marrowness!"

With that, the vicar fetched a knife and fork.

The Blunders looked on aghast, as he was about to burst their balloon!

"It's allergic!" cried Betsy.

"What's allergic?" asked the vicar.

"The marrow. It's allergic to vicars!"

"I have never heard such rot in all my life!"

He pushed his knife and fork into the "marrow".

"STOP!" cried Bunny.

"WHAT NOW?"

"Do you really want to murder this marrow?"

"Kill it?"

"It's got its whole life ahead of it. It might want to travel, see the world. And, of course, have baby marrows!"

"Baby marrows?"

"Yes, ickle baby ones."

The vicar became tearful. "Who am I to deny this marrow a future? I will never eat another vegetable in my life! Only animals from now on! Villagers! We have a winner!"

"NO!" exclaimed Farmer Farmer. He whipped off his cap, hurled it to the ground and stamped on it in frustration. His flat cap was even flatter than it was before.

"I think you stepped on your cap," said Bertie, picking it up, dusting it off and handing it back to him.

"The winners of the village marrow-growing competition are…"

Still holding on to their "marrow" to stop it floating away, the Blunders beamed at each other. They had got away with it.

"STOP!" boomed a voice.

The villagers looked around. Where was the voice coming from?

"STOP, I SAY!"

"THERE!" shouted Butler, pointing at the roof of Blunder Hall.

The airship pilot was dangling from the end of the cannon by one of the lines of his parachute.

"WHO ARE YOU?" cried the vicar.

"I AM A NAZI SPY!" replied the pilot.

"WHAT ARE YOU DOING UP THERE?"

"I WAS SHOT DOWN!"

"IN WHAT?"

"THE *BRATWURST*."

"YOU WERE FLYING A SAUSAGE?"

"NOOO! THE *BRATWURST* IS THE NAME

OF OUR LATEST WAR MACHINE. A DEADLY
AIRSHIP ARMED WITH MACHINE GUNS!"

"WERE YOU ON A MISSION?"

"A TOP-SECRET MISSION!"

"WHAT NOW-NOT-SO-TOP-SECRET MISSION?"

"TO FIND AN ENGLISH COUNTRY HOUSE
FOR THE FÜHRER TO LIVE IN AFTER HE HAS
INVADED!"

Bertie shook his head. "First the man from the bank
wants Blunder Hall. Then it's the Führer!"

"SO THERE IS GOING TO BE A WAR! HITLER
IS PLANNING TO INVADE!" shouted Old Lady
Blunder.

"THAT'S NOT IMPORTANT RIGHT NOW!"
replied the pilot hurriedly. "WHAT IS IMPORTANT
IS THAT THIS IS A DARK DAY FOR MARROW-
GROWING COMPETITIONS THROUGHOUT
THE WORLD! THAT IS NO GIANT MARROW!
IT IS IN FACT AN—"

VI

"Well, Vicar, that's settled, then!" interrupted Bertie. "We Blunders have triumphed! WE HAVE WON THE MARMALADE!"

"WHATEVER YOU DO, DON'T GIVE THOSE BLUNDERS THE MARMALADE!" shouted the pilot, swinging forward to make his point, "BECAUSE THAT IS NO MARROW, IT IS IN FACT AN..."

The parachute line snapped.

TWANG!

The pilot fell...

"ARGH!"

...landing in the Hook-a-Duck pond below.

SPLOOSH!

He spat a rubber duck out of his mouth.

"...AN AIRSHIP!"

he spluttered.

All eyes turned to the "marrow". Bertie and Betsy were still holding on to it.

"OOPS!" they said, turning to each other.

THE BLUNDERS WERE RUMBLED!

"Blunders," began the vicar, "this is a new low! Cheating in the marrow-growing competition indeed! You have brought shame on our village!"

"It's all my fault," said Bertie. "I thought for once we Blunders could be winners. But we are, and will always be, losers."

"Just like you British will be losers in the war!" exclaimed the pilot.

"NEVER!" thundered Old Lady Blunder. "AND WE WILL NEVER LOSE BLUNDER HALL! NOT TO THE BANK! NOT TO YOUR FÜHRER! NOT TO ANYBODY!"

"YES!" cheered the villagers.

Just then the pilot pulled out a pistol.

"Not so brave now, are you?" he sneered.

"CURSES! The one time I don't have my

blunderbuss!" cried Old Lady Blunder, still holding on to the airship.

"Keep holding on," hissed Brutus. "I have a plan. And, Bunny, I need your help!"

"Children! Careful!" whispered their mother.

"We will be," replied Bunny.

"Don't worry. I'll be their back-up!" whispered Old Lady Blunder.

The pair snuck off, leaving their fellow Blunders holding tight to the *Bratwurst*.

Meanwhile, the pilot stalked across the lawn, pointing his pistol at the villagers.

"NOBODY MOVE!" he ordered.

Butler was shuffling off back to the house, slower than a snail.

"NOT SO FAST!"

Butler put his hands up.

"And where do you think you are going?"

"Oh! Just to make a telephone call."

"To whom? The police? To raise the alarm?"

"Oh no!" lied Butler. "I was just going to wish my great-grandmother a happy birthday."

"How old is she?"

"Three hundred and two."

"A likely story! Get back!"

This diversion was all that the children and Old Lady Blunder needed.

Now they were on

the attack!

Brutus and Bunny were riding Cedric.

Brutus was holding the huge jar of marmalade, and Bunny was clutching a stick of candyfloss bigger than her.

"SQUAWK!"

The pilot spun round.

Old Lady Blunder performed a daring cartwheel, kicking the pistol out of his hand.

THWUCK!

"ARGH!"

Unable to stop, she flew into the coconut shy...

CLONK! CLONK! CLONK!

...knocking over every single coconut!

"BULLSEYE!" she cried.

Meanwhile, Cedric bounded over to the pilot.

Brutus hurled the marmalade over him.

SPLOOSH!

"URGH!" he cried, now glazed from head to foot in sticky orange goo.

But the worst was yet to come.

As Cedric circled, Bunny reached out her stick and coated him in candyfloss!

"NOO!" he cried.

The pilot now looked like a little pink cloud.

"HA! HA!" laughed the villagers as he lurched this way and that, searching for his pistol. As he bent down to pick it up, Betsy let go of the airship, leaving Bertie alone with it.

"Pegasus! CHARGE!" she cried, and galloped towards the pilot, holding her riding crop. Just as he was about to point his pistol, she whacked him on his marmaladed and candyflossed bottom with her riding crop.

THWACK!

"AH!"

The pilot stumbled towards the airship, waving his pistol at Bertie.

Bertie put his hands up in the air, letting go of the airship. As it floated away, the pilot grabbed on to the last rope dangling to the ground.

"DON'T LET HIM GET AWAY, BOY!" cried Old Lady Blunder.

But the pilot *was* getting away, and Bertie felt helpless to stop him.

"I'M GOING TO REPORT YOU ALL THE FÜHRER!" was the pilot's parting shot as he drifted up into the air.

"PAPAPAPAPAPA! STOP THE *BRATWURST*!" cried Bunny.

DING!

That gave Bertie an idea! If faced with a giant sausage, he would take a bite. So that's exactly what he did. He leaped into the air and bit the end of the *Bratwurst*!

CHOMP!

Air shot out so fast that the airship took off like a rocket.

Z O O M !

"HELP!" cried the pilot.
He held on tight, as
the giant sausage whirled
in the sky.

It went left.

It went right.

It went up.

It went down.

It zigzagged.

It looped the loop.

As the air spurted
out of the *Bratwurst*,
it made a rude noise,
like the world's
longest and noisiest
BOTTOM BANGER!

PFFFFFFFFFT!

The *Bratwurst*
hurtled up into space.

WHOOSH!

"HURRAH!"
cried the villagers.

The vicar addressed everyone. "THE BLUNDERS SAVED US ALL! LET'S GIVE THEM THREE CHEERS! HIP! HIP!"

"HOORAY!"

"HIP! HIP!"

"HOORAY!"

"HIP! HIP!"

"HOORAY!"

This made the Blunders glow with joy. For the first time in their lives, they were winners.

"SQUAWK!" squawked Cedric, bounding over to them with Butler riding on his back. As the bird bounded, he bumped villagers out of the way.

"OOF!"

"AH!"

"HUH!" they cried as they were walloped into the air.

"JOLLY GOOD SHOW, CEDRIC!" said Old Lady Blunder, patting the bird on his head. "AND JOLLY GOOD SHOW, BUTLER!" she added, patting the butler on his head.

The vicar appeared behind the group with a small jar of marmalade.

"The big one is gone, but please take this little one with all our thanks, Blunders!" he said.

"But we cheated," replied Bertie.

"You might not have won the marrow competition, but with your bravery, Blunders, you have won all our hearts."

"Thank you, Vicar. There is always next year's marrow-growing competition!"

"No," said the vicar. "I am giving you Blunders a lifetime ban."

"Oh!"

THE
MYSTERIOUS MYSTERY
OF THE
MISSING BUTLER

"BUTLER!" called Bertie. "BUTLER!"

His voice echoed around Blunder Hall.

Butler the butler was the most loyal butler. He had served the Blunders for decades without ever taking a day off. He had become part of the family in all but name. Whenever Butler was called, he would spring into action. Well, hobble into action these days.

However, on this particular morning, he was nowhere to be found.

Bertie called for the man another three hundred times, before finally giving up.

"BUTLER!"

Three hundred and one!

Not being the brightest sparks, the Blunders were not able to do much for themselves.

Bertie desperately needed Butler right now. It was an EMERGENCY! A TROUSER EMERGENCY! And that is the most serious emergency there is.

Bertie searched every inch of Blunder Hall for Butler:

- Behind the cushions on the sofa.
- In the gramophone.
- Under the carpet.
- Up the chimney.
- In the cutlery drawer.
- Under the ostrich.
- In all the pots and pans.
- Under the ashtray.
- Even in his coat pockets.

"You never know," muttered Bertie to himself, "he may have shrunk in the wash!"

Even though he looked in the unlikeliest places, Bertie couldn't find Butler.

So he gathered his family in the drawing room to see if they had any clues that could help to solve this mysterious mystery.

"BLUNDERS! ASSEMBLE!"

All the Blunders were missing Butler, but none more than Bertie.

"This morning I lost a button on my trousers! And then I lost my trousers!" he exclaimed as he stood there in his undercrackers.

"I pray Pegasus hasn't eaten your trousers," said Betsy. "If he has, I don't blame him. With Butler missing, there was nobody to serve breakfast. I haven't eaten a thing all day, and it's very nearly ten o'clock in the morning!"

"I don't know what I'll do if there isn't anyone to pick up my dirty socks!" wailed Bunny. "BOO! HOO! HOO!" she cried, spraying her fellow Blunders with her tears.

"I don't care if there's no one to clean this old ruin!" said Brutus. "I've always dreamed of living in total squalor!"

All eyes turned to the boy. What a grubby little fellow he was.

It just so happened that Old Lady Blunder was the last one to have seen Butler alive.

"This morning, I asked Butler to clean Blunder Hall inside and out. He set off with his brush, but I haven't seen a whisker of him since! Whatever could have become of him?"

The Blunders' suggestions came thick and fast.

"Butler was carried off by an army of ants!"

"He sneezed so hard he flew out of the window!"

"He had a very hot bath and because he is so old he turned into gravy and swirled down the plughole!"

"He fell through a crack in the floorboards!"

"While searching for coins down the back of the sofa, he tumbled forward and is trapped inside!"

"He sadly died, but then very kindly buried himself in the garden!"

On reflection, none of these seemed the least bit likely.

Old Lady Blunder was becoming tetchy. So tetchy that she raised her blunderbuss and fired it at the ceiling.

BANG!

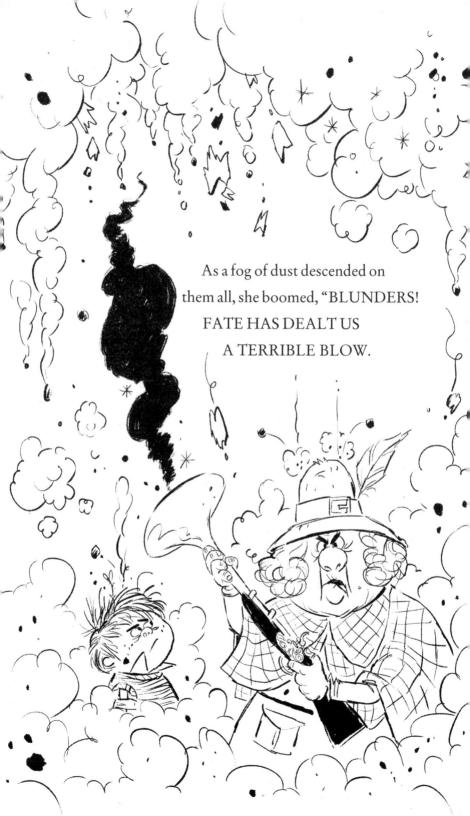

As a fog of dust descended on them all, she boomed, "BLUNDERS! FATE HAS DEALT US A TERRIBLE BLOW.

Butler has been missing for over an hour now! We have to pull together before Blunder Hall descends into chaos. We must do something we Blunders haven't done for generations!" She paused. "We must work!"

BANG! BANG! BANG!

"Mamamama?"

"Yes, Bertram?"

"I think you might be making more mess by firing at the ceiling."

"BALDERDASH!"

BANG! BANG! BANG!
BANG! BANG! BANG!
BANG!

II

"Oooooooooooohhhhhhhhhh!" exclaimed Bertie.

He was busy dusting the shelves with Cedric's bottom…

"SQUAWK!"

…when he suddenly remembered something. Something important.

"Darling! Whatever is the matter?" asked his wife, galloping in on her imaginary horse.

"I forgot!"

"Your name is Bertram Blunder. You live at Blunder Hall—"

"YES! YES! YES! I remember all that. But I almost forgot what I had forgotten. We have a busload of tourists about to arrive at the house!"

"Why?"

"I opened Blunder Hall to the public."

"Did you?"

"Yes!"

"Did it occur to you to tell anyone?"

"I forgot!" replied Bertie.

"Why have you done this? This is our home! Not a museum!"

"I know, but we need the money! Our time is running out! The man from the bank will be back in only two weeks, to turn Blunder Hall into Blunder blasted Borstal!"

B R U M M !

There was the sound of a bus approaching.

"SQUAWK!" squawked Cedric, alerting them to the sound.

"Oh no!" exclaimed Betsy. Her tummy gurgled loudly.

JURGLEMCFURGLE!

"What was that?" asked Bertie.

"You know I get an attack of the bottom burps whenever I'm nervous!"

"Oh no. Poor you. And poor us. Nevertheless, we need to get Blunder Hall spick and span in the next minute!"

"Darling, it's impossible!"

"We must! You see, I told a little white lie."

"You did?"

"Yes, to encourage them to come. I told the nice Norwegian gentleman on the telephone that this house is in fact a royal palace."

"Oh no!"

"It gets worse."

"It can't!"

"I also told him an absolute whopper."

"WHAT?" queried Betsy.

"SQUAWK!" went Cedric.

"That we are not the Blunders…"

"No?"

"No. That we are in fact… THE ROYAL FAMILY!"

KNOCK! KNOCK! KNOCK!

FUGROUBLE! went Betsy's tummy.

III

GURURGLE!

"Just my tummy again, darling!" said Betsy. "Find your trousers, and then answer the front door, and I will alert the rest of the Blunders! Good luck! You will need it!"

"Thank you, my love," replied Bertie.

KNOCK! KNOCK! KNOCK!

Betsy scuttled off sideways like a crab, clenching her buttocks together for fear of something unspeakable happening.

KNOCK! KNOCK! KNOCK! KNOCK! KNOCK! KNOCK! KNOCK! KNOCK! KNOCK!

There wasn't time to find his trousers. Instead, Bertie rushed to the front door and opened it. There was a large group of Norwegian tourists gathered outside. The men were strapping fellows with bushy blond beards. The women were tall too, with long blonde hair. It must be the VIKING BLOOD in their veins.

"Good afternoon! I am the Queen!" spluttered the trouserless Bertie. "I mean the King! Welcome to my royal palace!"

"Why aren't you wearing any trousers?" asked the burliest, beardiest one. He had a strong Norwegian accent and seemed to be the leader of the group.

"Oh, well, you see…"

"We are waiting!"

"I wanted this tour to be extra special. I mean, have you ever seen a king in his undercrackers?"

They all shook their heads.

"There you go! Now, please could I collect the royal entrance fee of one royal shilling from each of you now?"

"NO!" said the leader.

"No?"

"We will pay at the end of the tour! When we are sure this is the royal palace you told me about on the telephone!"

Bertie gulped. "Righto!"

There was no point in arguing with this mighty man and his mighty beard.

"If you really are the King, why don't you have a butler to answer the door for you?" asked another.

"Yes well, erm, um..."

"Well?"

"The royal butler was eaten alive by a badger this morning."

"We are all very sorry," said a lady, speaking for the group.

"Oh! These things happen! He'd had a good innings. Please enter our royal palace!"

The group trooped into Blunder Hall, not the least bit convinced that this was in any way royal.

"IT'S COLD."

"DAMP."

"DUSTY."

"DIRTY."

"AND SMELLY!"

"That'll be my royal undercrackers," replied Bertie. "They haven't been washed for a week! Now, please follow me, as we begin our royal tour! GULP!"

Meanwhile, all the other Blunders were taking in the extraordinary news in the library.

"THIS WILL BE A BREEZE!" exclaimed Old Lady Blunder. "Compared to us Blunders, the royal family are oiks!"

"I always knew I should be made a princess!" cooed Bunny.

"Being royal, can we imprison anyone we don't like in the Tower of London?" asked Brutus. Then he pointed at his big sister. "Guards? Take her away!"

"Children, your father is taking these visitors on a guided tour of the house. So be ready! Be radiant! Be royal!"

WURFURGURGLE!

"What on earth was that?" demanded Old Lady Blunder.

"Oh, nothing!" lied Betsy. "Come on, Blunders! If we pull this off, we could make a fortune! And Blunder Hall would be saved!"

"HURRAH!"

QURGLEMCFURGLETRUMTRUMMUNGLE!

"You look nothing like the King," remarked a tall lady who loomed over Bertie. "I've seen a photograph of him in the newspaper."

"Well," he replied, "when I go out and about on my official royal duties, I go in disguise. That way nobody recognises me."

This was met with baffled looks from the Norwegian tourists.

"THIS WAY!" said Bertie. "Let's begin with the throne room!"

He led them down the hall to the toilet.

"TA DA!" he said, swinging open the door.

"That's a toilet!" said a lady at the front.

"No! No! No! It's my brand-new invention, THE TOILET THRONE!"

"THE TOILET THRONE?"

"Yes! We royals are very busy people, and so we might need to open parliament and drop a doobry at the same time!"

Having convinced no one, Bertie hurried on with the

tour. "Now, who wants to meet the Queen?"

Like many upper-class twits, Betsy owned ballgowns and a tiara. So, when Bertie flung open their bedroom door, she greeted the visitors in all her finery.

BRUMFURGLOSTRICHLURGEVURGLE PUFLURGLE! went her tummy.

"Your Royal Highnessness, Your Majesty the Queen!" said Bertie.

"Yes, Your Most Royal Highnessnessness, Your Majesty the King?" she replied.

"I would like to introduce you to some charming visitors to our royal palace, who have come all the way from Sweden!"

"NORWAY!"

"Norway!"

The visitors all stared at this imposter, who looked as much like the real Queen as the biggest, beardiest man in the group.

"Charmed!" said Betsy.

"Well, lovely to finally meet you," replied Bertie.

There were mutterings from the Norwegians.

NO WONDER! How could the King only be meeting the Queen for the first time now? They must have met on their wedding day at the very least! THIS WAS ALL BONKERS! AND BANANAS! BONKERNANAS!

Bertie bowed to Betsy, and in return she performed an elegant curtsy. As she did, Betsy's worst nightmare came true. She let off the most explosive BOTTOM BANGER!

KABOOM!

The visitors were appalled. It was so deadly that the biggest, beardiest one fainted.

THUMP!

"OOPS!" said Betsy, glowing bright red.

"Now, all visitors to our royal palace plead to meet the delightful royal children," said Bertie as he led the group to the nursery. "I give you, the Prince and Princess!" he announced.

Bertie swung open the door to an anarchic scene. Brutus was riding Cedric around the room. The grubby little boy was holding the head of one of Bunny's dolls and laughing.

"HA! HA! YOU CAN'T CATCH ME!"

Bunny was wearing a bridesmaid's dress and a toy crown. She looked like a princess, even if she was not acting like one. She was standing on a pile of books attempting to lasso her little brother with her skipping rope.

"I'LL GET YOU, YOU ROTTER!" she was shouting.

"PRINCE! PRINCESS! PLEASE STOP THIS!" cried Bertie.

As usual, the pair completely ignored their father.

Instead of lassoing her brother, Bunny accidentally lassoed one of the Norwegian men by his beard.

"ARGH!" he cried in pain.

He was yanked off the ground and swung round the nursery.

WHIZZ!

He collided with Brutus and Cedric.

KABOOF!

"ARGH!"

"SQUAWK!"

Like a bowling ball, Brutus rolled across the floor towards the visitors.

TRUNDLE!

He knocked them over like skittles.

BOMPH!

"OUCH!"

BOMPH!

"OOF!"

BOMPH!

"OW!"

Any of the visitors who hadn't been struck by Brutus were walloped by a "flying" ostrich.

KERLUD!

"NOOOO!"

Any of the visitors who hadn't been struck by Brutus or walloped by the ostrich, were thumped by the man who'd been lassoed by his beard.

DOOOOF!

"YOUCH!"

Any of the visitors who hadn't been struck by Brutus or walloped by the ostrich or thumped by the man who had been lassoed by his beard, were walloped by Bunny, who had been whisked off the pile of books by the end of her lasso!

THWOCK!

"HUH!"

Now everyone, including Bertie, was lying in a huge heap on the floor.

Bertie was on the bottom, being crushed by some burly Norwegians. "Well, thank you so much, my darling little Prince and Princess," he said. "Now it's time to meet the Queen Mother!"

Once the Norwegian tourists had scrambled to their feet and dusted themselves off, Bertie led them down the corridor to Old Lady Blunder's study.

Inside, the national anthem was playing on the gramophone, and she was singing along.

"God save our gracious King!
Long live our noble King!
God save the King!"

Bertie listened from the other side of the door.

"They're singing about me again!" he said, then turned the door handle. "I give you, the Queen Mother!"

As the door opened, the most magnificent scene was revealed. Old Lady Blunder was sitting in the middle of the room, oozing royalty.

CHRISTMAS CRACKER
CROWN (CROWN)

FLY SWATTER
(SCEPTRE)

CRICKET
BALL (ORB)

SILK CURTAINS
(CLOAK)

DINING CHAIR
WITH THREE LEGS
(THRONE)

"Good day, Your Royal Highnessness the Queen Mother! It is I, your royal son, the King!" said Bertie. "May I and some paying visitors enter your most royal chamber?"

"You may, Your Majesty!" she replied in her poshest voice.

Old Lady Blunder was the only one who had the poise to pull this off. The visitors were instantly convinced. They all bowed their heads.

"I do hope you have had an agreeable visit to the royal palace today," she said.

"We have now, Your Royal Highness," replied the leader.

"Do I detect an accent?"

"Norwegian, ma'am."

"Every one of us has come all the way from Norway specially to visit this royal palace," added another.

Suddenly Old Lady Blunder's mood changed. "DID YOU COME IN A LONG SHIP?"

"Yes, it was quite long, ma'am."

"A VIKING SHIP?"

The visitors laughed. Bertie tittered nervously. But this was NO JOKE! Old Lady Blunder tore off her paper crown and curtain cape, before hurling her orb and sceptre across the room.

"YOU VIKINGS WAITED A THOUSAND YEARS TO MAKE A SURPRISE ATTACK!

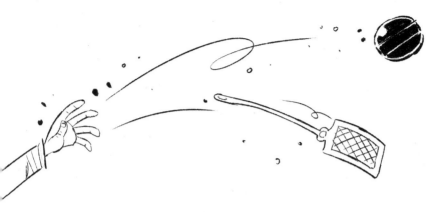

ONLY NOW HAVE YOU RETURNED TO PLUNDER OUR HOME! BLUNDERS! BATTLE STATIONS!"

"MAMAMAMAMAMAMA! NOOOOOOOO!" cried Bertie.

There was no stopping her!

"OUT OF MY WAY, YOU FOOLISH BOY!" she bellowed.

She stood up and reached for her blunderbuss.

"VIKINGS! PREPARE FOR THE BATTLE OF YOUR LIVES!"

"WE ARE NOT VIKINGS!" replied one of the visitors.

"YOU LOOK LIKE VIKINGS! YOU SOUND LIKE VIKINGS! YOU *ARE* VIKINGS!" thundered Old Lady Blunder.

She raised her blunderbuss and fired a warning shot over their heads.

BANG!

"ARGH!" they screamed in terror.

"OH! DON'T MIND MAMAMAMA!" cried Bertie. "SHE CAN BE RATHER SHOOTY!"

BANG! BANG! BANG!

The visitors fled as fast as they could.

"NOOO!"

They rushed down the staircase and straight out of the front door.

"THEY'RE GETTING AWAY!" thundered Old Lady Blunder. "BLUNDERS!"

The others stepped out into the corridor.

"What now?" asked Betsy.

"TO THE ROOF!"

"MAMAMAMAMAMA! PLEASE! NO!" pleaded Bertie.

But she marched up the stairs, her family trailing in her wake.

When they reached the roof, they looked down on a dramatic scene. The visitors were running alongside the

bus, attempting to jump on as it sped down the drive.

The bus had **VIKING TOURS** emblazoned on the side. Of course, it was just a playful name for a Norwegian holiday firm, but Old Lady Blunder didn't see it that way.

"VIKINGS! I KNEW IT!" she cried.

Old Lady Blunder tried to fire another warning shot, but her blunderbuss merely clicked.

CLICK! CLICK! CLICK!

"ROTTEN LUCK!" she shouted.

"Not for them," remarked Bertie.

"THE CANNON!" remembered Old Lady Blunder, stomping over to it. When the Blunders had caught up with her, a voice echoed from somewhere.

"HELP! I AM STUCK INSIDE HERE!" it said.

"What was that?" asked Brutus.

"It sounded like Butler!" added Bunny.

"I didn't hear a thing!" replied Old Lady Blunder. "But our Viking invaders are about to! HA! HA!"

With that, she spun the cannon, lit the fuse, and...

KABOOM!

...instead of a cannonball flying out, Butler did!

" *H H H E E E L L L P !* "

The poor man, dusted with soot and clutching a brush, was blasted towards the bus.

WHOOSH!

Old Lady Blunder was such a good shot that he landed on it.

CLUNK!

As the bus sped off into the distance, Old Lady Blunder shouted after him.

"BUTLER! COME BACK! YOU HAVEN'T FINISHED CLEANING OUT THE CANNON YET!"

THE
THRILLING BLUNDERWATER ADVENTURE

PLINK! PLINK! PLINK!

The Blunders awoke the next morning to a mysterious sound.

PLINK! PLINK! PLINK!

Something was plinking in Blunder Hall.

PLINK! PLINK! PLINK!

The noise echoed around the house.

PLINK! PLINK! PLINK!

It was so irritating that the Blunders couldn't think straight. Well, they never found it easy to think, let alone think straight, but this PLINK! PLINK! PLINK! made it impossible to THINK! THINK! THINK!

They needed to find where this plink was coming from!

After hearing a billion and one plinks, Bertie finally decided that enough was enough. He called a family meeting in the library.

"BLUNDERS! ASSEMBLE!" he cried.

Butler was on hand to serve some tea and biscuit. (There was just the one biscuit left in the tin.)

PLINK! PLINK! PLINK!

As the plink kept plinking, Bertie began: "BLUNDERS! Many of you may be aware that there is a plinking sound coming from somewhere in Blunder Hall!"

"BERTRAM! LANGUAGE, PLEASE!" thundered his mother.

"I said 'plinking'!"

"YOU JUST DID IT AGAIN!"

Bertie was perplexed.

Bunny made a lunge for the biscuit, and – not wanting to share it with her brother – scoffed it.

"Ha! Ha!" she snorted, spraying crumbs over him.

Brutus just stood there and smirked.

"Why aren't you annoyed?" asked Bunny.

"You'll find out soon enough," he replied.

"Oh! That biscuit tasted funny. Pruney!"

"Huh! Huh!" sniggered Brutus, his hands hidden behind his back.

"What have you got there?" demanded Bunny.

"Nothing!"

"You are hiding something!"

"No! I'm not!"

"Give it here!" said Bunny, snatching it. "It's my skipping rope! What were you doing with my skipping rope?"

"Nothing!"

"Please, children! We need to stop this plink!" said Bertie.

"I can hear a plink and so can Pegasus!" said Betsy, patting her imaginary horse.

"Daft as a brush," muttered Old Lady Blunder.

"Now," began Bertie. "This plink sounds like water dripping."

"Papapapapa, you're a genius!" said Brutus sarcastically.

Not understanding sarcasm, Bertie replied, "Why thank you. We need to find where this sound is coming from. So, Bunny and Brutus, you search the bedrooms and bathroom. My dearest darling Betsy?"

"Yes, my most darling of darlings?"

Brutus pretended to puke: "Bleurgh!"

"You search all the rooms on this floor. The kitchen, the dining room, the ballroom, the drawing room and the toilet! Mother?"

"What is it now, boy?"

"You search the loft. And, Bertie? BERTIE? Oh! I am Bertie! Silly me! I will search the cellar."

"If I might make a suggestion?" began Butler.

"FOR GOODNESS' SAKE, SPIT IT OUT, MAN! WE HAVEN'T GOT ALL DAY!" thundered Old Lady Blunder.

"It might be a dripping tap. Why don't I call a plumber?"

"A PLUMBER? *A PLUMBER?*" she bellowed. "WE BLUNDERS HAVE NEVER USED A PLUMBER BEFORE AND WE NEVER WILL! THE ONLY TOOL A PLUMBER NEEDS IS THIS!"

Proudly, she held her blunderbuss aloft, before stomping up the staircase to hunt this plink down.

"ONWARD!" she cried.

II

PLINK! PLINK! **PLINK!**

Bunny and Brutus began their search in the bathroom. This seemed the most likely place to find water dripping. But the taps weren't dripping, the pipes weren't dripping and the shower head wasn't dripping.

Still, they could both hear that PLINK! PLINK! **PLINK!** sound echoing around the room.

The only thing of interest Brutus found was a giant spider climbing out of the plughole of the bath.

His big sister hated spiders. So, while she was bent over inspecting the basin, he picked it up and tiptoed over to her. Then he placed it on the small of her back.

Any moment now she would shriek the house down!

Brutus watched as the spider crawled from Bunny's back on to her bottom.

Brutus sniggered.

"HUH! HUH!"

The spider might even bite her bottom!

However, no one could have predicted what happened next. Not even me, and I am making all this up.

You see Brutus had dipped that biscuit in FARTASTIC prune juice. That is why it tasted funny. And Brutus was sure the result would be hilarious.

It didn't quite work out like that.

Bunny was never one to break wind, but break wind she did!

TOOT!

The force of the blast shot the spider across the room.

W H O O S H !

Brutus's mouth was wide open in shock. So wide that the spider flew into his mouth.

THWUT!

It hit the back of his throat. He couldn't stop himself gulping.

GULP!

Brutus swallowed the spider whole.

"Pardon me!" said Bunny, turning round to see her little brother dead still with a troubled look on his face, his eyes crossed.

"Well, don't just stand there like a lemon, Brutus! Help me!"

"HELP *ME*!" he replied. "I'VE JUST SWALLOWED AN ENORMOUS SPIDER!"

"You've eaten far worse!"

"It's creeping down my gullet!"

"What do you want me to do about it?"

"Hold me upside down and see if you can shake it out!"

"WITH PLEASURE!" replied Bunny with a wicked grin.

She grabbed his ankles and began shaking him up and down.

"URGH! URGH! URGH!" cried Brutus. "It's not coming out!"

"Let me try something else!" she said, her eyes widening with delight.

Bunny began spinning her brother round by the ankles. Slowly at first, then she gathered momentum. Brutus spun faster. And faster! AND FASTER!

"Has it come out yet?"

"NO!"

She held on to him tightly, and spun him faster still.

It was too fast for her to keep control, and Bunny

found her feet lifting off the floor.

"NOOOO!" she cried.

But it was too late!

Now they were both spinning round the bathroom like a propeller.

WWWWWHHHHHIIIIRRRRRRRRRR!

To try to slow them both down, Brutus grabbed hold of the toilet seat.

Instead of making them stop, this wrenched the seat off the toilet.

GERTHUNK!

On the next revolution round the room, the toilet seat struck the toilet bowl.

KLANG!

The bowl cracked…

CRUNKLE!

…as the children landed in the bath.

DOINK!

"OOOF!"

"OW!"

They watched in horror as crack after crack spread across the toilet bowl like bolts of lightning.

CRUNKLE! CRINKLE! CRANKLE!

Then there was silence, before it SHATTERED!

TWUNK!

Water sprayed out of the hole where the toilet had been and on to the floor.

WHOOSH!

In moments, the water was so deep that the bath began to float before drifting off.

"NOOOOOOOO!" cried Bunny.

"YES!" exclaimed Brutus.

III

Downstairs, Betsy was galloping through Blunder Hall on her imaginary horse. She was bolting from room to room in search of the plink.

Butler was in the kitchen when Betsy rode in.

"STEADY, PEGASUS!"

"Oh! Good afternoon, your ladyship," he said as he inspected the sink taps.

"Have you got a sugar lump for Pegasus, please?"

Butler rolled his eyes and found the sugar bowl.

"How should I feed it to him, your ladyship?"

"Just pop it in Pegasus's mouth!"

Butler went to do that.

"WRONG END, SILLY!" she said.

Butler sighed and shuffled over to where the other end might be. He lifted the sugar lump to the horse's mouth, let go and of course it just dropped to the floor.

DONK!

"BUTTER FINGERS! So, Butler, is this dripping

sound coming from the kitchen?"

"It doesn't appear so, no!"

"But I can still hear that PLINK! PLINK! PLINK!"

"Me too."

PLINK! PLINK! PLINK!

Water began seeping from the bathroom floor down into the kitchen.

"LOOK!" shouted Betsy.

"Oh dear."

"It's just water, Pegasus! Don't be spooked!"

The imaginary horse must have bucked, because Betsy began bouncing up and down.

"WHOA THERE! BUTLER! HELP!"

"What can I do?"

"GRAB THE REINS, MAN!"

Butler reached out to grab some air, but it was too little too late.

Betsy somersaulted across the kitchen, landing in the sink with a CLUNK!

Her weight pulled the sink off the wall.

K E R L U N K !

"NO!" cried Butler.

He shuffled over as fast as he could to catch it, but the

sink fell and smashed on the floor…

CRASH!

…yanking the pipes with it.

CLANG!

Water began spurting out of them.

SPLOOSH!

Butler tried to stop the jets, but the force of them pushed him back.

SPLOOSH!

In no time, the water in the kitchen was knee-deep.

"Naughty horse!" remarked a soaking-wet Betsy.

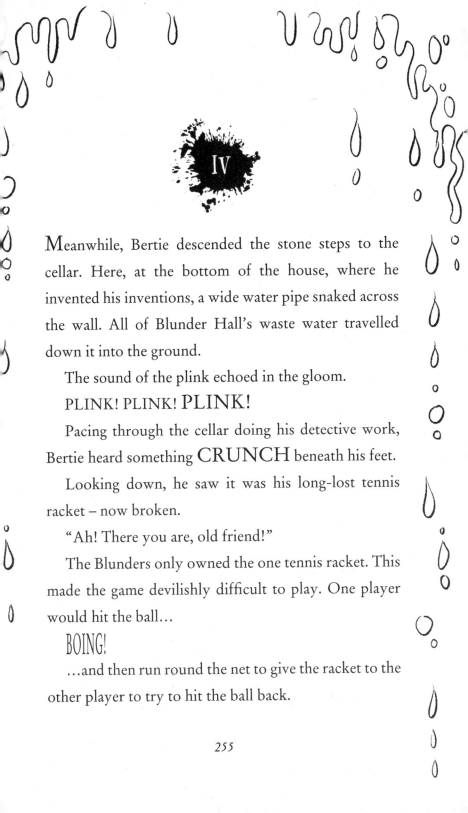

Meanwhile, Bertie descended the stone steps to the cellar. Here, at the bottom of the house, where he invented his inventions, a wide water pipe snaked across the wall. All of Blunder Hall's waste water travelled down it into the ground.

The sound of the plink echoed in the gloom.

PLINK! PLINK! PLINK!

Pacing through the cellar doing his detective work, Bertie heard something CRUNCH beneath his feet.

Looking down, he saw it was his long-lost tennis racket – now broken.

"Ah! There you are, old friend!"

The Blunders only owned the one tennis racket. This made the game devilishly difficult to play. One player would hit the ball…

BOING!

…and then run round the net to give the racket to the other player to try to hit the ball back.

BOING!

And so on and so forth.

Oh, and they played with a cricket ball.

Bertie called this game "crennis". Like all his inventions, it never caught on.

Stumbling in the dark, Bertie kicked something. It trundled across the floor.

TRUNDLE!

"The ball!" he exclaimed. "Let's see if I could still be a crennis champ!"

He whacked the ball against the wall.

THWACK!

It struck the water pipe hard…

TONK!

…smashing a hole in it.

Instantly, water spurted out of it!

SPLURT!

"Oops!"

Oops indeed! Soon the water in the cellar was knee-deep.

If that wasn't enough disasters for one day, Bertie could feel drips of water landing on him.

DRIP! DRIP! DRIP!

He placed his tennis racket over his head to act as an umbrella. Unfortunately, the strings let the water through.

"Blast!"

Suddenly, the drips became a downpour!

SPLOOSH!

Water from the kitchen above gushed down into the cellar.

Now the water in the basement was waist-deep.

The ceiling began to crack...

CRACKLE!

...before the entire thing caved in...

BOOF!

...bringing Betsy, Butler and the kitchen sink with it!

All plunged into the deep water below.

SPLASH!

The sink sank, but Betsy and Butler's heads bobbed above the surface.

"Super day for a swim!" chirped Bertie.

"I never knew we had a pool down here," said Betsy.

"Ahem!" began Butler, who was looking up through the hole. Now the bathroom floor above the kitchen was

buckling under the weight of water. "If I might draw your attention to the kitchen ceiling for one moment."

"Butler! I am just practising my backstroke!" replied Bertie.

"Is there a diving board?" asked Betsy.

The ceiling caved in.

GERRUNK!

The bath began falling.

"BATH INCOMING!" shouted Butler, pushing the lord and lady out of the way.

The bath, with Bunny and Brutus still in it, landed
in the cellar with a huge *S P L O S H !*

"Oh! Hello, children!" said Betsy brightly. "What
brings you all the way down here?"

"A bath," replied Brutus.

At the top of the house, Old Lady Blunder was stalking the drip with her blunderbuss.

PLINK! PLINK! PLINK!

The attic was low-ceilinged, so nobody could stand up in it. It was the ideal place to conceal yourself in a game of hide-and-seek, if you didn't mind crouching indefinitely.

As she pushed open the door, Old Lady Blunder could hear that the noise was louder than ever.

PLINK! PLINK! PLINK!

BINGO!

The sound was coming from above.

PLINK! PLINK! PLINK!

There was a small skylight in the ceiling.

PLINK! PLINK! PLINK!

When she looked up, Old Lady Blunder realised that the plink wasn't a drip, after all.

PLINK! PLINK! PLINK!

Something was tapping on the glass of the skylight. That was what was making this sound!

PLINK! PLINK! PLINK!

The plinks were being made by...

PLINK! PLINK! PLINK!

...AN OSTRICH!

Cedric was tapping on the glass with his beak.

PLINK! PLINK! PLINK!

Not being able to fly, he was trapped on the roof. He was trying to get back into the house!

PLINK! PLINK! PLINK!

When Cedric saw Old Lady Blunder staring up at him through the skylight, he flapped his wings nervously. However, as much as he wanted to fly off to safety, it was impossible. Ostriches can't fly.

"DO NOT FEAR! OLD LADY BLUNDER IS HERE!" she shouted. The skylight was far too small for an old lady or indeed an ostrich to fit through. So she had a daring but dangerous plan.

"MOVE ASIDE, CEDRIC!"

As the bird hopped out of sight, Old Lady Blunder did what she always did to solve a problem: FIRE HER BLUNDERBUSS!

Lying flat on the attic floor, she blasted a big hole in the ceiling.

BANG! BANG! BANG! BANG! BANG!

As the smoke cleared, Cedric looked down through the hole as Old Lady Blunder looked up.

"COME TO GRANDMAMAMAMA!"

"SQUAWK!" went the bird, shaking his head. He didn't trust her with that thing.

"WELL THEN! GRANDMAMAMAMA WILL COME TO YOU!"

Old Lady Blunder heaved herself up and popped her head through the hole. As she was still holding the blunderbuss, the ostrich took several paces back towards the edge of the roof.

Cedric's feet slipped, and a tile was dislodged.

CLATTER!

It hit the ground below with a KERUMP!

"SLOWLY! SLOWLY! CATCHY OSTRICH!"

At once the pair were locked in a dance, circling each other. After a few times round the roof in both directions, Old Lady Blunder knew she had to change tactics.

She took a running jump and landed on the bird's back!

THUMP!

"SQUAWK!"

Her weight was too much for Cedric. He stumbled through the hole, taking Old Lady Blunder with him!

"SQUAWK!"

"ARGH!"

Their combined heft meant they crashed through the attic floor.

KERUNCH!

"SQUAWK!"

Then fell through the hole in the bathroom floor.

KERUNCH!

"SQUAWK!"

Fearing the worst, Cedric covered his eyes with his wings!

Then they fell through the hole in the kitchen floor.

KERUNCH!

"SQUAWK!"

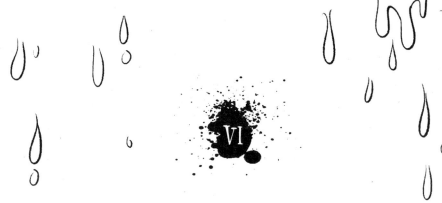

Old Lady Blunder and Cedric's fall was broken when they landed on the others floating in the bath.

KERCLONK!

Well, it used to be a bath; it was now doubling as a boat.

"Mamamama, welcome to my bathboat!" exclaimed Bertie.

"Bathboat?" she spluttered.

"Yes! My brilliant new invention! Bathe while you cruise! We could make millions! Pay off the bank and then all sail around the world in it!"

KNOCK! KNOCK! KNOCK!

"There's somebody at the door," said Butler. "Should I swim over and answer it?"

"No, Butler!" replied Old Lady Blunder. "STAY HERE! WE NEED YOU TO PADDLE!"

Butler did his best, attempting to navigate the bathboat through all the floating furniture.

KNOCK! KNOCK! KNOCK!

"OPEN UP, BLUNDERS!" came a voice.

"It's the man from the bank!" cried Bertie.

"Stall him!" said Old Lady Blunder.

"Just a moment, please! We are dealing with a tiny plumbing issue!"

"Poppycock!" replied the man from the bank. "Open this door at once! I am here with the bailiffs! We are going to impound all your antiques!"

"They are all in pieces!"

"Anything that isn't in pieces, then! The silverware, the chandeliers, even the brass doorknobs!"

"But how will we open the doors?"

"That is no concern of mine – you should have read the small print! Now open this door, or bailiffs will break it down!"

KNOCK! KNOCK! KNOCK!

Now there was so much water in Blunder Hall that the bathboat was floating all the way up from the cellar to the ground floor!

"That plinking wasn't a dripping tap or any such nonsense like that," said Old Lady Blunder. "It was Cedric here, tapping on the skylight in the roof to get back in. PLINK! PLINK! PLINK!"

Cedric nodded his head.

"How did he get all the way up there?" asked Bunny.

"He fell?" guessed Bertie.

With his beak, Cedric pointed towards Brutus.

"SQUAWK!"

The boy smirked.

KNOCK! KNOCK! KNOCK!

"THAT LITTLE STINKER DID IT!" cried his big sister.

"BOG OFF, BUNNY!"

"The question is, how did Cedric end up on the roof?" asked Butler. "Ostriches can't fly!"

"I used Bunny's skipping rope to pull down a huge branch of a tree to the ground. I tricked Cedric into stepping on the branch by scattering some ostrich biscuits on it, and then I let go! He crash-landed on the roof!"

Cedric's eyes crossed in fury as he nodded his head.

"The next question is, why?"

"I wanted to see if I could make an ostrich fly!"

"If you were my grandson," began Old Lady Blunder, "I would put you over my knee!"

"I am your grandson," said Brutus.

"So you are. Well, I don't have time right now, but later please remind me."

"Of course I will!" lied Brutus.

"I won't forget, Grandmamamama!" said Bunny.

KNOCK! KNOCK! KNOCK!

"If I might interject…" began Butler.

"FOR GOODNESS' SAKE, MAN! SPIT IT OUT!" thundered Old Lady Blunder.

"Perhaps the more pressing issue is how to save us all from drowning!"

Now the water in Blunder Hall had risen so high that the bathboat had floated up towards the top of the house.

Soon there would be no escape!

BLUNDER HALL UNDERWATER

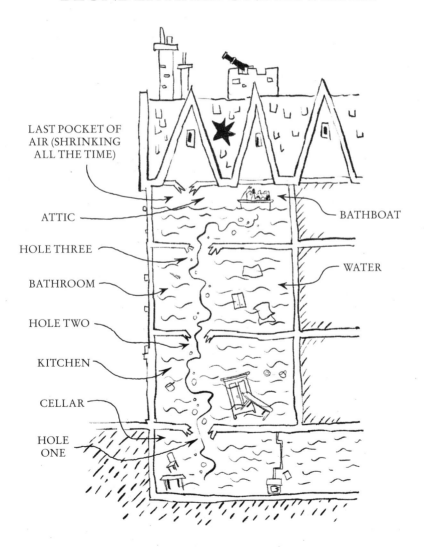

LAST POCKET OF
AIR (SHRINKING
ALL THE TIME)

ATTIC

HOLE THREE

BATHROOM

HOLE TWO

KITCHEN

CELLAR

HOLE
ONE

BATHBOAT

WATER

One fact about ostriches that may have escaped your notice is that although they can't fly they can SWIM!

As heads bumped the ceiling, the pocket of air getting smaller and smaller, Cedric dived off the bathboat.

"What is that silly bird doing now?" asked Bunny.

Cedric popped his head out of the water and gestured to the others to follow.

They had no choice! As they were being squashed against the ceiling, they leaped off the bathboat.

SPLOSH! SPLOSH! SPLOSH! SPLOSH! SPLOSH!

They took one last gulp of air, before grabbing hold of Cedric's feet. The bird looked round to check everyone was holding on tight, before diving down. Cedric powered through the water.

Down,

down,

down.

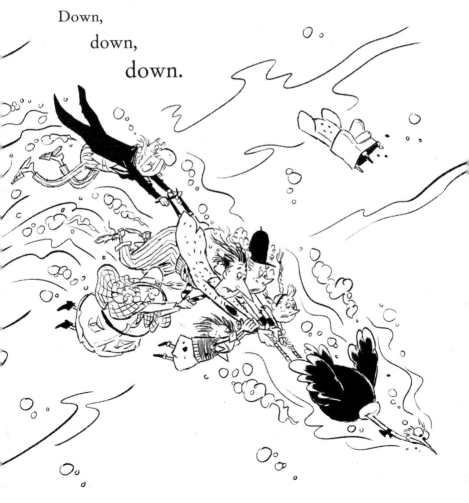

Soon the Blunders had reached the front door.

KNOCK! KNOCK! KNOCK!

"RIGHT! THAT'S IT! BAILIFFS! BREAK

DOWN THE DOOR!"

A battering ram smashed it open...

KERRASH!

...and water began whooshing out.

SSSPLLLOOOOOOOOSHHH!

The Blunders, Butler and Cedric were swept out, right into the man from the bank and his brutish bailiffs.

The rushing river carried everyone along the drive.

The Blunders grabbed hold of some trees, but the three baddies were flushed through the gates.

"I'LL BE BACK!" shouted the man from the bank, his head bobbing in the water.

"MISSING YOU ALREADY!" shouted Bertie as he held on to a branch.

THE
BLUNDERS' BOARD GAME

All was cold. All was white. All was silent.

Thick snow had fallen on Blunder Hall.

The snow was so deep that the front door opened on to a wall of white.

The Blunders were all trapped inside the house – and there was only a week to go until the man from the bank would be back.

They were running out of schemes to save Blunder Hall.

A Christmas family tradition was to play games. Of course, the Blunders being Blunders, these games would end in disaster.

HIDE-AND-SEEK was a favourite, but with the Blunders this could take weeks to play. That's because they would forget who was doing the hiding and who was doing the seeking. One Christmas Day they all ran off to hide:

Old Lady Blunder in a suit of armour.

Bunny in the grand piano.

Brutus in the toilet. Or, rather, down the toilet, with only his head poking out of the pan.

Cedric in a biscuit tin. Well, his head was hidden in it. That way he could scoff all the biscuits. "SQUAWK!"

Bertie under a pot plant. Well, he stood there balancing a pot plant on his head.

Butler in a chest of drawers, and he had a well-earned nap. "ZZZ! ZZZZ! ZZZZZ!"

And Betsy behind her invisible horse.

A week went by with everyone doing the hiding and no one doing the seeking.

It was only when Butler woke up in need of a pee, that anyone realised.

I-SPY works best when the players know the first letter of words.

Over the years the Blunders had been shocked to discover that:

OSTRICH doesn't begin with a P.

TWIT doesn't begin with an H.

PEGASUS doesn't begin with a Z. This was always going to be an impossible one to guess, as the horse is imaginary, and therefore invisible, making it devilishly difficult to spy.

Once the family had finally established that BLUNDER begins with a B, which was news to all of them, that was now the thing they spied EVERY SINGLE TIME.

"I spy with my little eye something beginning with B..."

"Blunder?"

"Yes!"

"I eye with my little spy something that begins with a B?"

"Is it Blunder?"

"Correct!"

"I eye with my little eye..."

"BLUNDER?"

"How did you know?"

GRANDMAMAMAMA'S FOOTSTEPS was Old Lady Blunder's favourite game. Of course, she was the grandmamamama, and everyone else had to creep up behind her. However, as always, Old Lady Blunder liked to add an element of DANGER.

This grandmamamama was armed with a BLUNDERBUSS!

As soon as she heard the first footstep, she fired a warning shot at the ceiling.

BANG!

As dust and debris exploded into the ballroom, the family fled.

CHARADES always went wrong for the Blunders. That's because none of them could remember the name of any book, film, song or play!

They had:

- *POOH THE WINNIE*
- *BELLS BELLS JINGLE JINGLE*
- *OZ OFF THE WIZARD*
- *BOOTS IN PUSS*
- *HALL OF TOAD TOAD*

MUSICAL CHAIRS might be a staple of any children's party, but the Blunders had their own version.

MUSICAL CHAIR. That's because there was only one chair in Blunder Hall on which it was safe to sit.

Many were broken. Others wobbly. There was a chair that had just three legs. Another just two. One had just one. But that still beat the one chair with no legs. Or seat. Or back. That was barely a chair at all.

As the music on the gramophone stopped, all the Blunders would charge at the one chair. That too would be broken, and the game would be over in a flash.

However, this passion for games gave Old Lady Blunder an idea.

"WE ARE BLUNDERS!" she began. She was addressing her fellow Blunders in the drawing room. "Now, Blunders begins with a B! I know that from our games of I-SPY! And do you know what else begins with a B? Grit! And do you know another word that begins with a B? Determination! Us Blunders have oodles of both. So, my fellow Blunders, let's make all the money we need to save our house by inventing our own game!"

"HURRAH!" cried the others.

Each Blunder devised their own game.

Old Lady Blunder created BLUNDERBUSS BINGO.

Not owning a bingo cage from which to draw bingo balls, she had to improvise. So she scrawled numbers on ping-pong balls, and fired them from her blunderbuss.

BANG! BANG! BANG!

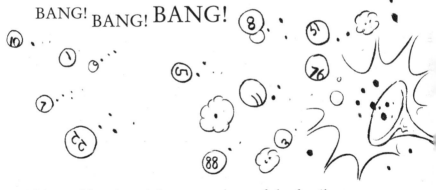

To avoid serious injury, members of the family were forced to use their bingo cards as shields.

DOINK! DOINK! DOINK!

Betsy named her game ROCKING HORSE JUMPING.

The horsey lady set up her horse jumps all around Blunder Hall. Next, she leaped on Bunny's rocking horse and tried to propel herself along the course. By the next morning, Betsy had only moved forward a few inches.

Having dreamed up so many inventions over the years, Bertie thought creating a game would be a doddle. CONNECT FOUR HUNDRED AND FORTY-FOUR was all his idea.

This was much like the modern game of CONNECT FOUR, but on a gargantuan scale, with a rack the size of a football pitch and thousands of coloured tokens.

Sadly, CONNECT FOUR HUNDRED AND FORTY-FOUR was impossible to play. You needed a crane to get high enough to drop your token through a slot.

All this time, Brutus was picking his nose and making a big ball of bogeys for his game, which he called BOGEYBALL. It was much like DODGEBALL,

 but instead of a rubber ball you hurled a huge green sticky icky ball of bogeys.

The problem was that the bogey ball was so sticky it remained stuck to your hand.

Bunny, being Bunny, came up with a game she thought only she could win.

It was BESTEST BALLERINA.

Bunny made them all compete against her in a ballet dance-off!

Bunny was sure she would be crowned winner, until it was discovered that Cedric was a world-class ballet dancer!

"SQUAWK!"

"NOT FAIR!" she cried, stamping her feet.

Butler watched all these games descend into chaos before he made a suggestion.

"If you will indulge me for a moment, I have thought of a game. There is—"

"WELL, DON'T JUST STAND THERE, MAN!

SPIT IT OUT!" thundered Old Lady Blunder. "OUR HOME IS AT STAKE!"

"As there is never a dull moment at Blunder Hall, I wonder if we could all work together to create a game based on life in this house!"

The Blunders were intrigued.

"Go on," urged Bertie.

"The board would be a map of Blunder Hall. There would be counters of each of you and of course a die. You roll the die and move forward spaces through the rooms of this house. The aim of the game is to make it all the way to the end of the board without the house falling down!"

"THE BLUNDERS' BOARD GAME!" exclaimed the Blunders all at once.

"IT'S A WINNER!" added Bertie.

III

Bunny and Brutus worked together on the board itself. It was the cover of an old atlas that had long ago lost all its pages. They drew the rooms and the squares before colouring them in. For the first time in yonks, the grown-ups didn't hear a peep out of the pair.

Betsy created the counters. Each one represented someone in the house. These figures were made from papier-mâché before being painted. Betsy took the most time over the one of Pegasus so it was especially pretty.

Bertie was tasked with making some CHANCE CARDS. If you landed on a red square on the board, you had to pick up one of these cards and do what it said. He scribbled on the back of a deck of playing cards.

These were just some of the Chance Card instructions:

YOU ARE ENJOYING A BATH WHEN IT CRASHES THROUGH THE FLOOR. **MOVE BACK A SPACE.**

YOUR WIFE'S IMAGINARY HORSE BOLTS. **MOVE HER COUNTER FORWARD TEN SPACES.**

YOU NEED A PEE DURING THE NIGHT, BUT ARE TOO IDLE TO WALK TO THE LAVATORY. INSTEAD, YOU PEE OUT OF THE WINDOW. YELLOW SNOW GIVES THE GAME AWAY. **GO BACK TO THE START.**

A SPACE-TIME PORTAL OPENS AND BLUNDER HALL IS TRANSPORTED BACK MILLIONS OF YEARS TO WHEN DINOSAURS RULED THE EARTH. A TYRANNOSAURUS REX EATS THE HOUSE AND EVERYTHING IN IT. **MISS A TURN.**

By the end of the day, THE BLUNDERS' BOARD GAME was ready to play. Once tried and tested, it would be ready to unleash on the world!

It was too obvious for the Blunders to play as themselves.

Instead, they would play as each other!

So Old Lady Blunder was Betsy.

Betsy was Brutus.

Brutus was Bunny.

Bunny was Bertie.

Bertie was Old Lady Blunder.

Pegasus was Cedric.

Cedric was Pegasus.

Old Lady Blunder rolled the die. It was really her leather hatbox with numbers painted on the side.

CLONK!

"A six!" she exclaimed, moving her Betsy counter forward by six spaces. "One! Two! Three! Four! Five! Five! Six!"

Because she'd counted five twice, Old Lady Blunder moved her counter seven spaces. Everyone was too terrified to correct her in case she fired her blunderbuss. She moved from the front door on the board, and into the dining room. As bad luck would have it, she landed on a red square! That meant she had to pick up a CHANCE CARD! She struggled to make out her son's handwriting at first, but then read out loud:

"YOU GUZZLE AN ENTIRE CRATE OF CHAMPAGNE. THE BUBBLES GIVE YOU AN ATTACK OF THE BOTTOM BURPS. THEY ARE SO FIERCE YOU TAKE FLIGHT! YOU ZOOM AROUND BLUNDER HALL AT LIGHTNING SPEED! MOVE FORWARD A DOZEN PLACES!

Ha! Ha! I love this game!"

The Blunders' Board Game was an instant hit! All the family loved playing it, and were sure that millions of others would too.

"Now we need to take our game to a board-game manufacturer!"

"Oddington's make most of the famous ones," suggested Butler.

"ODDINGTON'S IT IS!" agreed everyone.

With that, Bertie put on his heaviest coat and opened the front door. He was greeted by the wall of white.

"Oh dear! I forgot all about the snow! And time is running out. We need to send off our genius invention right away. BLUNDERS! TO THE ROOF!"

V

Soon the Blunders, Butler and Cedric were wading through the thick snow on the roof. After some time, Bertie reached the cannon.

"Which way is Oddingford?" he asked.

"That way!" replied Old Lady Blunder, pointing.

Bertie began turning the cannon so it was facing the right way.

He pulled out a pen and wrote on the box.

*Top Secret!
For the attention of
Mr Oddington only!*

Then he placed the game into the end of the cannon.

"Mother! Light the fuse!" he ordered.

"GLADLY!" she replied.

Butler spoke up: "Sir, are you sure this is a good—"

But before he could say "idea" there was the

loudest noise.

BANG!

The cannon fired, and the game shot high in the air.

WHOOSH!

As it did so, it caught fire from the gunpowder sparks!

WHOOMPH!

It flew like a flaming phoenix before crumbling into a thousand pieces. These tiny grey wisps fluttered down to earth, landing on the deep snow as dust.

"Oops!" exclaimed Bertie.

The Blunders shuffled back downstairs in silence.

They were sad. Butler was sad. Cedric was sad. If Pegasus had existed, he would have been sad too.

That was until Butler piped up. "Excuse me, Blunders, but I just had a thought. What if you played THE BLUNDERS' BOARD GAME for real?"

"WHATEVER DO YOU MEAN?" demanded Old Lady Blunder. "COME ON, MAN! DON'T DILLY-DALLY! SPIT IT OUT!"

"Well, each of you dresses as someone else in the family, and instead of moving around the board, why not move around the house?"

"HURRAH!" shouted the Blunders.

The family merrily swapped clothes.

In no time, Bertie was dressed as Betsy.

Betsy was dressed as Brutus.

Brutus was dressed as Old Lady Blunder.

Old Lady Blunder was dressed as Bunny.

Bunny was dressed as Bertie.

Cedric dressed in Butler's uniform, and Butler did his best to protect his modesty with an ostrich feather.

Looking at each other, they all burst into fits of laughter.

"HA! HA! HA!"

It was a moment of light comedy. Little did the Blunders know that they were about to face a dark and deadly DRAMA.

THE
TERRIFYING TALE
OF
TIDDLYPOPS

It was the dead of night. Blunder Hall was quiet. The only sound was the deafening foghorn of Old Lady Blunder snoring.

"ZZZ! ZZZZ! ZZZZZ!"

She was laid out like a queen on her four-poster bed – well, it used to be four, but it was now a one-poster bed. Tonight, as every night, Old Lady Blunder cuddled her blunderbuss as if it were a teddy bear. That's why she now had a one-poster bed, because when she'd been fast asleep she'd blasted three of the posts off when her finger accidentally squeezed the trigger.

BANG! BANG! BANG!

Old Lady Blunder had slept through the whole thing.

"ZZZZZZZZZZZ!"

She went to bed with her blunderbuss in the unlikely event of:

- A full-scale military invasion by the Welsh.
- Her twin sister making a surprise visit.
- A herd of wildebeest stampeding through Blunder Hall.
- The police banging on the door to arrest her for not having a licence for her blunderbuss.
- A fly buzzing around her bedroom.
- Most importantly, the man from the bank returning to convert Blunder Hall into a borstal!

Now, Blunder Hall's grandfather clock couldn't count – much like its owners. In fairness to the grandfather clock, that wasn't its fault. It was so ancient it could barely move its arms.

So at two o'clock it might chime eleven times, or at seven o'clock it might chime once. I don't need to go on and on explaining, or this book would become unspeakably long and boring.

Tonight, the grandfather clock did something it rarely did. At midnight it chimed thirteen times.

TWONG! TWONG! TWONG! TWONG! TWONG! TWONG! TWONG! TWONG! TWONG! TWONG! TWONG! TWONG! TWONG!

On the thirteenth chime, a ghostly apparition took shape at the end of Old Lady Blunder's bed. It looked like a cat, except it was transparent and glowed. It opened its mouth and bared its long, sharp fangs.

"HISS!"

The dead had come back to life! This was a miracle! But not the miracle anyone would wish for!

Old Lady Blunder felt this presence. She sat bolt upright in her bed. She spied this terrifying thing and opened fire.

'Shoot first! Ask questions later!' was always her motto. It was one that she believed had served her well, despite the unfortunate death of her husband.

BANG! went the blunderbuss.

The bullet passed right through the phantom!

"*HISS!*"

The creature leaped off Old Lady Blunder's bed and scrambled out of her room.

Old Lady Blunder bounced out of bed.

"THE HUNT IS ON!" she said to herself.

She stormed out of her bedroom. The phantom was running down the stairs towards the front door. Old Lady Blunder gave chase, blasting all the way.

BANG! BANG! BANG!

Ornaments exploded. Paintings were shot off the wall. Furniture splintered into a thousand pieces. All these possessions that Butler had painstakingly glued back together after the last disaster were in bits again.

The phantom darted towards the front door. Halfway down the stairs, Old Lady Blunder took aim and fired.

The phantom passed straight through the door just as it was blasted off its hinges. The door fell to the ground with a...

THERUNT!

The BANG, BANG, BANG, BANGs woke up everyone in Blunder Hall.

As Cedric squawked wildly and hopped up and down...

"SQUAWK! SQUAWK! SQUAWK!"

...the Blunders charged down the staircase towards Old Lady Blunder.

Bunny stamped her foot. "What is all this hullabaloo?"

"The noise was so loud I could barely hear my own bottom bangers!" moaned Brutus.

"Mamamamama! I would much rather you didn't fire that thing indoors," said Bertie.

"It frightens the horses!" added Betsy, who had been sleeping in her full riding outfit, including hat and boots.

Finally, Butler the butler shuffled into view, wearing his nightgown and cap.

"Does someone need a hot-water bottle?" he asked.

"No, Butler! Not now!" thundered Old Lady Blunder.

"You know this house better than anyone. You have been here longer than any one of us!"

"That is true, my lady. It is my belief that Blunder Hall is… HAUNTED!"

Macabre music played.

DUM! DUM! DUM!

All eyes turned to the grand piano.

Cedric was banging the keys with his beak.

"SQUAWK!"

"Let me tell you a terrifying tale. MURDER AT BLUNDER HALL," began Butler. "Many years ago—"

"Sorry!" interrupted Bertie. "I hate to be a party pooper, but I desperately need a pee. Do you mind speeding it up a bit, Butler?"

"There's a ghost. The end!"

"Mmm, that was a trifle too fast."

After pees had been peed, and poos had been pooed, the Blunders gathered around the fire in the drawing room. There, Butler shared with them the terrible secret he had been keeping from them for decades.

"Hundreds of years ago, the then Lord Blunder owned a beautiful black cat, as fearsome and beautiful as a panther. Her name was Tiddlypops! Tiddlypops couldn't have been more devoted to her master. She followed Lord Blunder everywhere: around the garden, into the village, even across Russia to do battle with the Ottoman Empire."

"Cool cat!" said Brutus.

"She survived the war, even if the Ottoman Empire didn't."

"So how did Tiddlypops die?" asked Bunny.

"She's dead?" exclaimed Bertie. "So young!"

Old Lady Blunder shook her head. "Excuse my son, Bertram. He is stupider than that ostrich!"

Cedric flapped his wings in protest. "SQUAWK!"

"Will there be any horses in this story?" asked Betsy.

"No," replied Butler.

"I'll go back to bed then! Giddy up, Pegasus!"

"SIT BACK DOWN!" ordered Old Lady Blunder. Betsy dismounted her imaginary horse and did what she was told.

"Butler! You never told us how Tiddlypops died," said Bunny.

"The lord fell in love with a lady. A lady who despised cats."

"WHY?" asked Bunny.

"As a child, she loved to yank cats' tails. One day, a cat struck back. It bit her on the bottom."

"OUCH!" said Bertie. "My second-least-favourite place to be bitten!"

"The love between her and Lord Blunder grew strong," continued Butler, "and one day they were married. The new Lady Blunder loathed Tiddlypops on sight. To try to starve her, she would scoff all her cat food!"

"YUCK!" exclaimed Bunny.

"YUM!" exclaimed Brutus.

"Is cat food actually made of cats?" asked Bertie.

His mother huffed at her silly son with his silly question.

"HUMPH!"

"Tiddlypops would get her revenge by piddling in Lady Blunder's shoes. This threw the woman into a fury. That night, she grabbed Tiddlypops by her tail! Then she stuffed her into a sack. Next, she leaped on her horse and rode through the night until she reached the river..."

"Oh no!" exclaimed Betsy. "I think I know what is coming next!"

"They were both hit by a meteorite."

"No. I was not expecting that."

"Legend has it that the ghost of Tiddlypops has haunted Blunder Hall ever since."

"What a coincidence!" remarked Bertie. "Only the other night, I saw a transparent ghost cat with a nametag that read Tiddlypops disappear through a wall. Do you think that could have been Tiddlypops?"

"BERTRAM!" exclaimed Old Lady Blunder. "Why didn't you say something at the time?"

"How was I to know it was important?"

"A GHOST IN BLUNDER HALL!" cried Betsy. "NOT JUST A GHOST! A GHOST CAT! This could be HUGE! Even bigger than the show-jumping championships I organised last year on the lawn!"

"That was a huge disaster!" scoffed Old Lady Blunder. "How can you have show-jumping championships without a horse?"

"In fairness, that was the one single element that was missing!" replied Bertie.

"A ghost cat could make us rich! Rich! Rich! RICH!" said Betsy. "We could pay off the man from the bank, save Blunder Hall and still have enough left over to build Pegasus a stable!"

"My darling, you are a genius like me!" exclaimed

Bertie. "Everyone loves ghosts, and most people love cats! Folk will come from all over the world to visit Blunder Hall!"

"For our very own...GHOST-CAT HUNT!" said Betsy.

III

Bertie rushed to the telephone. He called up newspapers all over the world to place advertisements.

ROLL UP! ROLL UP!

WELCOME TO THE WORLD'S FIRST EVER GHOST-CAT HUNT! ONLY AT BLUNDER HALL.

A GHAT (OR COST) HUNT AWAITS YOU AT BLUNDER HALL!

DIE OF FRIGHT OR YOUR MONEY BACK.

ARE YOU A **CAT PERSON** AND ALSO A **GHOST PERSON**? THEN BLUNDER HALL'S

GHOST-CAT HUNT

IS YOUR PERFECT NIGHT OUT.

Soon the Blunder Hall telephone was ringing all day and all night with people of all nationalities wanting to book for the Ghost-Cat Hunt.

RING! RING! RING! RING! RING! RING! RING! RING! RING! RING!

As the Blunders were celebrating their good fortune, Bunny had a thought.

"How do we know when the ghost of Tiddlypops might appear? You can't have a ghost-cat hunt without a ghost cat."

The Blunders scratched their heads. Even the wise old butler had no idea.

Fortunately, Cedric saved the day. The ostrich hopped over to the grandfather clock.

"SQUAWK!"

"LOOK!" said Butler. "Cedric is trying to tell us something!"

Standing beside the grandfather clock, the bird leaped up and down and squawked thirteen times.

"SQUAWK! SQUAWK! SQUAWK! SQUAWK! SQUAWK! SQUAWK! SQUAWK! SQUAWK! SQUAWK! SQUAWK! SQUAWK! SQUAWK! SQUAWK!"

"Is it some kind of ostrich Morse code?" guessed Old Lady Blunder.

"I heard thirteen squawks!" said Butler.

Cedric nodded his head. The ostrich opened the door with its beak, and headbutted the gong.

TWONG!

"Thirteen! Chime!" said Butler, trying to solve the riddle. "I've got it!"

"WELL, SPIT IT OUT, MAN!" ordered Old Lady Blunder.

"Thirteen chimes!"

Cedric nodded his head.

"SQUAWK!"

"The ghost of Tiddlypops only appears when the clock strikes thirteen!"

"SQUAWK!"

"PERFECT!" said Bertie. "We just need to wait until thirteen o'clock!"

"LOOK AT THE CLOCK FACE, BERTRAM!" ordered his mother. "IS THERE A NUMBER THIRTEEN?"

"How am I supposed to know that?"

"All we need to do," began Butler, "is make the clock

strike thirteen times and the ghost cat will appear right on cue!"

"BONGO!" exclaimed Bertie. "I mean BINGO!"

THE GHOST-CAT HUNT took place the very next night at midnight. Thick fog had enveloped Blunder Hall. It was spooky. It was scary. It was sinister.

The perfect night to step into THE UNDERWORLD OF THE UNDEAD.

Butler was standing at the door to greet the visitors.

Betsy was sitting in the hall with a tin bucket, ready to take all the much-needed money.

Old Lady Blunder was holding her blunderbuss, ready to blast anyone who didn't cough up.

Bunny and Brutus had been installed behind the grandfather clock to make it chime thirteen times. But only when given the signal!

Bertie had not been assigned a task, as that was thought to be for the best. So he loitered behind his wife, trying to look useful.

A hundred or more people had gathered outside the front door.

KNOCK! KNOCK! KNOCK!

The door, which had been stood back up and wedged into place after being blasted off its hinges, toppled over into the hall.

T H U M P !

"WELCOME TO BLUNDER HALL!" announced Butler. So accustomed was he to opening the front door to guests, that his hand reached out for the door handle, which wasn't there. "YOU MUST BE HERE FOR THE GHOST-CAT HUNT! PLEASE ENTER… IF YOU DARE!"

The visitors were already spooked as they stepped over the front door into the house. All were very much cat people, as they had brought their cats with them. Or perhaps the cats had brought their owners. We will never know.

"One shilling each for the ghost-cat hunt, please!" announced Betsy. Spotting all the cats, she saw an opportunity. "And an extra shilling for your cat."

"I am not sure cats carry money!" whispered Bertie, loitering behind her like a spare part.

One by one, the visitors dropped their money into the bucket.

CLUNK! CLANK! CLINK!

However, the last man in the queue created quite a conundrum. On top of his head was sitting a cat. The man had clearly combed and parted its fur to look like his hair.

It was the world's worst wig.

When Betsy asked him for the extra shilling for his cat, the man went scarlet with fury.

"I don't have a cat!" he barked.

"THEN WHAT'S THAT THING SITTING ON YOUR HEAD?" demanded Old Lady Blunder, brandishing her blunderbuss.

"MY HAIR!" replied the man.

"IT LOOKS AN AWFUL LOT LIKE A CAT TO ME!"

"WELL, IT'S NOT!"

"IS!"

"NOT!"

"IS!"

"NOT!"

Old Lady Blunder tricked him by saying. "NOT!"

"IS!" he replied. "NOOO!"

"WAKE UP, KITTY! KITTY! KITTY!" she said, poking its bottom with the end of her blunderbuss.

Instantly, the cat woke up.

"MIAOW!"

"SEE? IT JUST MIAOWED!" exclaimed Old Lady Blunder. "NO ENTRANCE WITHOUT THE EXTRA SHILLING!"

"HARUMPH!" he replied, dropping a coin in the bucket.

CLANK!

"I have never been more insulted in my life! And neither has my cat! I mean wig! I mean hair!"

The man rushed to catch up with the group. As he broke into a jog, he passed a saucer of milk up to his hair.

"There you go, Mr Fluffy!"

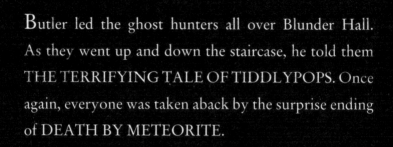

Butler led the ghost hunters all over Blunder Hall. As they went up and down the staircase, he told them THE TERRIFYING TALE OF TIDDLYPOPS. Once again, everyone was taken aback by the surprise ending of DEATH BY METEORITE.

After an hour or so of trooping round and round Blunder Hall in the early hours of the morning, the visitors were becoming twitchy.

"THIS IS A SWIZZ!"

"IT'S A PACK OF LIES!"

"THERE WAS NO METEORITE!"

"I BET THERE WAS NO TIDDLYPOPS!"

"WE WANT OUR SHILLINGS BACK!"

"AND THE SHILLING SURCHARGE FOR OUR CATS!"

"MIAOW!" miaowed all the cats in agreement.

Mr Fluffy, still perched on his owner's head, hissed malevolently.

"*HISS!*"

"WHEN ARE WE GOING TO SEE THIS GHOST CAT?" cried the visitors.

"Within moments," replied Butler.

It was his plan all along to make them wait. Build up the tension.

Butler winked at Betsy, who winked at Cedric, who winked at Old Lady Blunder, who winked at Bertie, who rather gave the game away by shouting "NOW!" at his children, who were STILL hidden behind the grandfather clock.

There was an awkward pause as Bunny and Brutus fought over who would set the clock off.

"MY TURN!"

"NO, MINE!"

"I HAVEN'T EVEN HAD A GO YET!"

"I ONLY HAD ONE GO AND YOU SPOILED MY GO BY HAVING YOUR OWN GO!"

"GET YOUR HANDS OFF MY GONG!"

"IT'S NOT YOUR GONG!"

"IT *IS* MY GONG!"

"I'LL GONG YOU IN A MINUTE!"

Butler called to the family pet to help. "CEDRIC!"

The ostrich opened the door of the grandfather clock with its beak and headbutted the gong.

TWONG! TWONG! TWONG! TWONG! TWONG! TWONG! TWONG! TWONG!

TWONG! TWONG! TWONG! TWONG!
TWONG!

At first there was silence. Then there was a sound of tinkling from above.

TINKLE! TINKLE! TINKLE!

Everyone looked up.

Dangling by his tail from the chandelier was THE GHOST CAT!

"MIAOW!" he cried down at the visitors.

Tiddlypops bared his long, sharp fangs and hissed. This was the fiercest hiss that had ever been hissed in the whole HISSTORY OF HISSINGDOM.

"HHHHHHHHHHHHHIIIIIIIISS SSSSSSSSSSSSS!"

The visitors and their cats shrieked in terror!

"AAAAAAAAAAAAAAAAAAAAA AAAAAAAAAAAAAAAAAAAAA AAAAAAAAAAAAAAAAAAAAA AAH!"

THE GHOST CAT was such a startling sight that all the cats went BANANAS!

They raced round and round in circles.

WHIZZ!

Clawed their way up the curtains.

SCRATCH!

They leaped up on to the furniture, knocking vases to the ground.

KERASH!

Burrowed under the rugs.

DIG!

Swept their owners off their feet.

WOOMPH!

Mr Fluffy leaped off his owner's head and landed on Cedric's back. The ostrich reached round and pecked the cat.

PECK!

"MIAOW!"

"SQUAWK!"

Mr Fluffy tried to swipe Cedric with his claw.

"HISS!"

A running battle between the two species raged around Blunder Hall.

It was not just pandemonium, but

CATDEMONIUM!

Meanwhile, the bald man was going CUCKOO! His not-so-secret secret was a secret no more!

"NOOO! COME BACK, MR FLUFFY!"

As the rushing river of cats swept by, he reached down and grabbed one.

"RIAOW!"

He flopped it on his head.

This cat, a hairless sphinx, protested wildly.

"RIAOW!"

So the man had to hold the sphinx cat in place with both hands. Not that it created any illusion of having a head of hair, as the cat was balder than he was, and he was TOTALLY BALD!

"YOU ARE NOT GOING ANYWHERE!" he said.

"*HISS!*" went the cat.

It bit into his finger.

CHOMP!

"YEEOUCH!"

The pain was eye-watering. The bald man let go and the cat leaped off his head.

Its claws pinged out and it landed on the silk curtains, ripping them to shreds as it slid down.

RIP!

"I WILL NOT HAVE BLUNDER HALL DESTROYED BY CATS!" bawled Old Lady

Blunder. She shot at the chandelier hanging from the ceiling in the hall. Tiddlypops was still dangling from it.

BANG!

"BULLSEYE!" she shouted as the chandelier and the ghost cat plummeted to the ground.

KERASH!

The ghost-cat hunters and their cats fled for their lives!

"ARGH!"

"HELP!"

"RUN!"

"RIAOW!"

They all raced out of the house, pursued by the ghost cat.

"HISS!"

The bald man snatched the bucket full to the brim with money from Betsy.

"WE'RE ALL TAKING OUR MONEY BACK!" he shouted as he too escaped into the night.

All the Blunders, plus Butler and Cedric, rushed to the door to watch them charge up the drive, chased by Tiddlypops.

Just then, the most unexpected thing happened.

A METEORITE ZOOMED DOWN FROM OUTER SPACE!

WHOOSH!

I told you it was unexpected.

IT CRASH-LANDED RIGHT ON TOP OF TIDDLYPOPS!

BOOM!

The impact with the Earth was so great that Blunder Hall shook.

KERUPPLE!

Anything in the house that hadn't crashed to the floor took this opportunity to do so.

SMISH! SMASH! SMOSH!

"Oh dear, oh dear," remarked Bertie.

"At least that is the last we'll see of Tiddlypops!" said Betsy.

It was now very nearly two o'clock in the morning. As the big hand on the grandfather clock clonked into place, it began to chime.

TWONG! TWONG! TWONG!

Everyone turned to face the clock.

TWONG! TWONG! TWONG!

This was so tense it was intense.

TWONG! TWONG! TWONG!

How many chimes would there be?

TWONG! TWONG! TWONG!

"Twelve chimes!" exclaimed Bunny. "We're safe!"

There was a collective sigh of relief, until…

TWONG!

In a flash, Tiddlypops reappeared, sitting on top of Bunny's head.

"HHHHHHHHHHHHIIIIIIIISSS SSSSSSSSSSSSSSS!"

"AAAAAAAAARRRR RRRRRGHHHHHH HH!"

THE
GREAT KNICKER CAPER

"A CIRCUS?" spluttered Bertie.

"YES!" exclaimed Betsy, bouncing up and down on their bed with excitement.

BOING! BOING! BOING!

"We can save our home with THE BLUNDER CIRCUS!"

Some ideas are barmy.

Others are bonkers.

But this was BANANAS!

However, the man from the bank was due to return at the stroke of midnight to demand the ten thousand pounds they owed. If the Blunders couldn't pay up, they would lose Blunder Hall forever.

This was their LAST CHANCE!

*

That morning, Betsy charged into the dining room on Pegasus and shared her plan.

"When I was a little girl, my mamamamamama and papapapapa took me to the circus for my birthday! The thrills! The skills! The jests! Aside from my papapapapa being eaten by a lion, it was the most magical day of my life. Everyone loves the circus! We could make a ton of money! And we desperately need a TON OF MONEY!"

"WE DO!" cried the Blunders.

As usual, Butler was the only voice of reason.

"I do not want to be a party pooper," he began, "but circuses require a great number of speciality acts. Where would we find those? Acrobats, clowns, jugglers, magicians, animals…"

"We Blunders will be the circus acts!" Betsy replied.

"HURRAH!" cried the Blunders.

"Pegasus could be the star of the show!" she continued, but only Betsy hurrahed this time.

"Hurrah!"

"Ma'am, where will we find a circus tent?" asked Butler.

"We will make one!"

"What from?"

"KNICKERS!"

"Knickers?"

"KNICKERS!"

"Mamamamamama, why do you keep saying 'knickers'?" asked Bunny.

"Because, my darling, we can make the big top from DRAWERS! BLOOMERS! FRILLIES! UNMENTIONABLES! PANTALOONS! UNDYWUNDIES! HONKER HANKIES! WALONKERS! TOGGLEDOBBLES! MINKIES! GRUNKLES! DOODLEPIPS! NICKYNACKYNOONAHS!"

"Mamamamama," began Brutus. "How many pairs of bloomers do you own?"

"Just the one!"

"Well, we can't make a circus tent from one pair of bloomers!"

"They are stretchy!"

"Still!"

Bunny shook her head. "We would need hundreds of pairs of bloomers to make a Big Top. How on earth can we find that many?"

"SIMPLE, CHILD!" replied Old Lady Blunder. "WE NICK THE KNICKERS!"

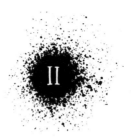

II

Old Lady Blunder's plan was simple. And COMPLETELY CUCKOO!

The Blunders would pedal their rusty old Rolls-Royce, the Baroness, around the local village. Riding on the roof would be Cedric. As they sped through gardens, the ostrich would pluck every last pair of bloomers from the washing lines. When they had enough pairs, they would race home and get sewing to make their Big Top.

The Blunders piled into the car, with Old Lady Blunder at the steering wheel. The engine had long since died so the car worked on PEDAL POWER! Four sets of bicycle pedals had been fitted. The only member of the family who did not have to pedal was Betsy. She was to sit in the boot collecting the bloomers that were passed to her by Cedric.

They waited until noon, when washing was likely to be out to dry, and people were likely to be inside having their lunch.

Butler the butler waved goodbye at the front door of Blunder Hall as the Baroness crashed through the gates…

K E R R A N G !

…and rumbled off towards the village.

The Blunders were in luck! Bloomers were hanging from every washing line! They were there for the taking like apples on a tree.

The car tore through hedges…

K E R R U N C H !

…and rolled over gardens, straight towards the washing lines. Once the unmentionables were within reach, Cedric lifted his long neck and snapped his beak on to a pair.

SNAP!

They were plucked off the washing line…

TWANG!

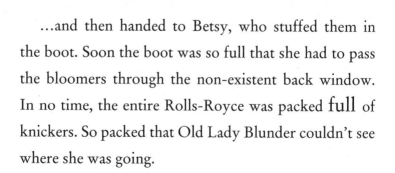

…and then handed to Betsy, who stuffed them in the boot. Soon the boot was so full that she had to pass the bloomers through the non-existent back window. In no time, the entire Rolls-Royce was packed full of knickers. So packed that Old Lady Blunder couldn't see where she was going.

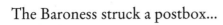

The Baroness struck a postbox...

CLUNK!

...ran down a road sign...

CRACK!

...and bounced off a telephone box.

BOING!

Finally, it plunged into the village pond!

S P L O O S H !

"HELP!"

"NOOO!"

"ARGH!" cried the Blunders.

Even Cedric, who was on the roof, let out a terrified

"SQUAWK!".

"KEEP CALM, BLUNDERS!" ordered Bertie as water began flooding into the car.

"BARONESS! PEDALO MODE!"

He pressed a special red button on the dashboard.

SUCCESS!

The tyres inflated to bursting and fins popped out of the side of the car.

THE BARONESS WAS NOW A CARBOAT!

"My latest invention! The pedalomobile! Now pedal, Blunders! Pedal faster than you've ever pedalled before!"

The Blunders pedalled furiously, and the only Rolls-Royce pedalo in existence powered through the pond.

S W O O S H !

Soon the Baroness reached the safety of the village green.

Old Lady Blunder pulled a pair of knickers off her face.

"WELL DONE, BLUNDERS!" cried Bertie.

"Bertram, I never thought I would say this, but you have finally invented something useful! I am proud of you, my boy," said Old Lady Blunder.

"Oh, thank you, Mamamamamamama!" replied Bertie.

"Now home!" cried Betsy. "We have a Big Top to make out of knickers!"

Have you ever tried to make a circus tent out of hundreds of pairs of knickers?

I have. Only a handful of times. But, let me tell you, it is no easy feat!

Butler found the sewing box. It had a dozen needles and a mile of thread. For the next few hours, the Blunders sewed and sewed and sewed. Finally, the family had made the biggest tent you have ever seen (unless you have seen a bigger tent made of bloomers in your life, in which case you can ask for a refund on this book).

The KNICKER TENT was erected, and sawdust was scattered on the grass to make a ring.

Posters were put up all over the village, advertising

THE BLUNDERS PRESENT...

THE BLUNDER CIRCUS!

THE 379TH
GREATEST SHOW
ON EARTH!

SUNDAY NIGHT AT BLUNDER HALL.
BOOK EARLY TO GUARANTEE
DISAPPOINTMENT.

Betsy already owned a red tailcoat, britches and riding boots as she spent most of the day sitting astride her imaginary horse. So, she assumed the role of RINGMISTRESS, welcoming the audience and introducing all the acts.

A trapeze act is a staple of any circus. It is not just thrilling but beautiful too, like dancing in the air. Bunny bagsied this act for herself. BUNNY'S TRAPEZE EXTRAVAGANZA was born. She did not rehearse once, though, believing that she was an expert at everything without even trying.

Bertie chose juggling.

First, he tried juggling with three balls and, instantly, he dropped them all.

BOING! BOING! BOING!

Then he tried with two balls. They suffered the same fate.

BOING! BOING!

Next, he tried with one ball. This proved to be impossible too.

BOING!

Finally, he tried to juggle with no balls. YES! At last, this was something he could master.

His act was named… BERTIE THE NO-BALLS JUGGLER!

Brutus loved circus acts that were deadly dangerous, so he began preparing to be BRUTUS THE STUNT BOY.

He constructed a GLOBE OF DEATH out of bits of old wood. The globe was for stunt motorcyclists to perform tricks inside it. However, the Blunders didn't own a motorbike. So Brutus had to make do with a penny-farthing.

A PENNY-FARTHING

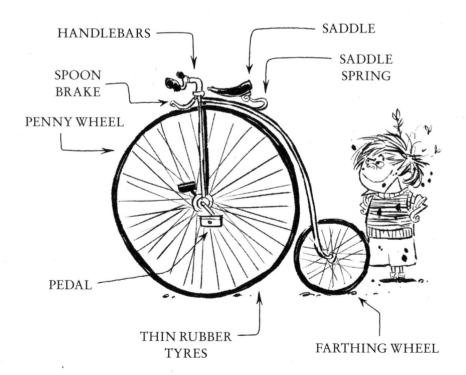

HANDLEBARS

SADDLE

SADDLE
SPRING

SPOON
BRAKE

PENNY WHEEL

PEDAL

THIN RUBBER
TYRES

FARTHING WHEEL

Butler was no clown, but he had to become one for the night:

BUTLER THE MILDLY AMUSING CLOWN.

Bunny raided her mother's make-up box and painted the old man's face.

He looked more like a trifle than a clown.

Butler knew that clowns made their entrance in a clown car – a car that collapses when you drive it. The Baroness was perfect for this!

THE WORLD'S FIRST FLYING OSTRICH sounded like a wonderful act.

Betsy was sure it would be the STAR ATTRACTION of THE BLUNDER CIRCUS.

Cedric was not so sure.

"SQUAWK!"

Especially when he saw the cannon from the roof of Blunder Hall being wheeled into the Big Top tent. He flapped his wings to fly away. But then the ostrich remembered he couldn't fly. After all, this was the whole point of the act.

"Don't fret, Cedric!" said Betsy, placing an old tin helmet on his head. "YOU WILL BE THE STAR OF THE SHOW!"

"SQUAWK!"

That just left Old Lady Blunder. She insisted that her act be the GRAND FINALE of the circus. But she wouldn't tell anyone what her act was. All anyone knew

was that she went missing from Blunder Hall for the afternoon as she needed to fetch something.

Everyone was nervous, waiting for OLD LADY BLUNDER'S STUPENDOUS SURPRISE!

That evening, the Blunders, plus Butler and Cedric, waited in the garden, excited for their show to begin. They peeked through a flap in the knicker tent, watching the audience take their seats for THE BLUNDER CIRCUS.

"LOOK!" said Bertie. "It's the man from the bank!"

Indeed, it was. He was sitting in the front row, checking the time on his gold pocket watch with a smug look on his face. A stern pair of police constables flanked him.

"He's early!" exclaimed Betsy.

"Only by a few hours. Blunder Hall becomes the bank's at midnight tonight. I bet that little rotter just can't wait to get his hands on our home!"

"We Blunders must put on the performance of our lives! Show that little squirt what we are made of!"

"HURRAH!"

"If only a million people come to the circus, we can still save our home!"

"DOUBLE HURRAH!"

Bunny sniffed the air.

"What's that revolting smell?" asked Bunny.

Now everyone sniffed the air.

"DOOBRIES!" exclaimed Brutus. He knew the smell of doobries better than anyone. "And not ostrich doobries!"

Cedric nodded his head in agreement.

He sniffed at Old Lady Blunder and pointed at her with his beak.

"Grandmamamamamamama?" said Bunny. "Why do you smell of doobries?"

"Don't spoil the surprise, child!" replied Old Lady Blunder with a wink.

"IT'S SHOWTIME!" said Betsy.

"WELCOME TO THE BLUNDER CIRCUS!" cried Betsy, galloping in on Pegasus. She went round and round the ring, whacking her own bottom with a riding crop.

The man from the bank crossed his arms and shook his head.

"What nonsense!" he muttered to the pair of policemen, who chortled.

"Ha! Ha!"

"THE FIRST ACT TONIGHT IS MY HUSBAND, LORD BLUNDER, BERTIE THE NO-BALLS JUGGLER!" announced Betsy.

There was a dramatic stab of music from the gramophone as Bertie bounded into the ring. Then he did all the things a juggler would do, except there were no balls! He hurled all nine no balls up in the air and caught them behind his back. He balanced all the no balls on top of each other on his nose. He even juggled all nine no balls with one hand! Without doubt, Bertie was the **greatest** no-balls juggler in the land. However, this failed to impress the audience.

"RUBBISH!"

"A JELLYFISH COULD JUGGLE BETTER THAN YOU!"

"OFF!"

"JUGGLE THIS!" shouted a wag from the back. And he hurled a Scotch egg towards Bertie.

WHIZZ!

Incredibly, Bertie managed to catch it.

In his mouth!

"HOORAY!" cried the crowd.

"THROW IT BACK, THEN!" shouted the wag.

Bertie took a bite from the Scotch egg, which got a good laugh.

CHOMP!

"HA! HA!"

Then he threw the Scotch egg back. But it hit the man from the bank instead.

Bang on the nose.

BOINK!

"OUCH!"

"HA! HA! HA!"

"SORRY!" said Bertie. He nodded to his wife, who hurriedly introduced the next act.

"NOW IT'S TIME FOR DANGER! MY SON, BRUTUS, AND HIS GLOBE OF DEATH!"

That was Bertie's cue to roll in the great wooden structure for their son.

T R U N D L E !

He opened the hatch on the side of the globe, and Brutus rode into the ring on the penny-farthing.

"How is he going to get that great thing in there?" shouted someone.

This was something Brutus had missed.

A penny-farthing is far too big to fit into a Globe of Death.

Instead, the huge front wheel knocked into it.

DONK!

The force threw Brutus over the handlebars.

W H O O S H !

"AHH!"

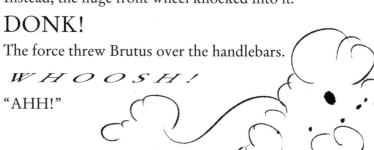

He landed on top of the globe. Scrambling to his feet, Brutus stood on top of it. Wobbling there, he moved his feet and tried to balance in fear of falling off.

The globe rolled forward…

TRUNDLE!

…straight towards the man from the bank!

Seeing that he was about to be run over by the Globe of Death, the man from the bank cried, "STOP!"

But Brutus couldn't stop!

He rolled over the man, the hatch open, and the man from the bank was trapped inside, like a hamster in a ball.

"LET ME OUT!"

"HA! HA! HA!" laughed the crowd, as the globe ran over the policemen who had been running to save him.

"Oh dear!" said Betsy. "Oh dear, oh dear! I'm terribly sorry. I'm sure we will have you out in a jiffy!" Then she turned to the audience. "BUT NOW IT'S TIME TO TITTER WITH BUTLER THE MILDLY AMUSING CLOWN!"

"I SAID LET ME OUT! NOW!"

There wasn't time, because BUTLER THE MILDLY AMUSING CLOWN had pedalled the Baroness into the ring. Not having a brake, the Rolls-Royce crashed into the Globe of Death.

CLONK!

"NOOOO!" cried the man from the bank.

The globe collapsed into pieces, as did the car.

The wheels fell off.

The doors fell off.

And the shell split into two.

Butler was left sitting on the sawdust, holding the steering wheel.

"HA! HA! HA!" laughed the audience.

The man from the bank was furious.

"HELP ME UP, YOU FOOLS!" he shouted at the policemen. They heaved him to his feet, and placed him back on his seat.

"HARUMPH!" he huffed, sweeping sawdust off his precious bowler hat.

"NOW PLEASE WELCOME THE QUEEN OF THE TRAPEZE! BUNNY BLUNDER!" said Betsy.

Bunny swept into the ring in her ballet outfit to polite applause.

She climbed the rope ladder to the top of the Big Top. Confident in her abilities, though never having practised once, she grabbed hold of the swing. Not being able to do anything but hold on, Bunny swung from side to side, slowly coming to a stop.

"ARE YOU ALL RIGHT UP THERE?"

"NO, MAMAMAMAMAMAMAMAMAMAMA!" she

replied, dangling in the air like a chimpanzee hanging from a tree.

"HOLD ON!"

"I CAN'T FOR MUCH LONGER!"

Her father, mother and little brother began climbing the rope ladder as fast as they could to rescue her.

"NEVER FEAR!" cried Bertie. "THE BLUNDERS ARE HERE!"

Bunny was now holding on by her little fingers! And even they were slipping!

"HHHEEELLLP!" she cried.

"HOLD ON, DARLING!" shouted Betsy.

But Bunny couldn't! Her fingers slipped! She fell!

W H O O S H !

"ARGH!"

V

From the ground, Butler looked on in terror. He was standing next to the cannon, Cedric's head poking out of the end.

"Cedric! You are our only hope!" he said, lighting the fuse.

FIZZLE!

The brave bird nodded his head.

"SQUAWK!"

"SAVE OUR BUNNY!"

BOOM! went the cannon. Cedric shot out.

W O O M P H !

"ARGH!" cried Bunny, plummeting to the ground.

Butler's timing could not have been more perfect!

Bunny landed on Cedric's back!

THOMP!

Now the audience weren't just watching a flying ostrich – they were watching a flying ostrich with a girl flying on top!

They rose to their feet at this amazing feat! Even the pair of policemen.

"BRAVO!"

THE BLUNDER CIRCUS WAS THE GREATEST SHOW ON EARTH!

The only person not giving the Blunders a standing ovation was the man from the bank.

He sat with his arms folded, grumpily refusing to clap.

Cedric and Bunny hit the side of the Big Top.

WALLOP!

With no more oomph from the cannon, they both began falling. Bunny gripped her legs round Cedric and grabbed hold of the tent.

"I'VE GOT YOU, CEDRIC!" she cried.

They tumbled down, taking a wall of knickers with them.

RIP!

The threads holding the knickers together split.

As the Big Top began to collapse, hundreds of pairs of knickers fluttered down on to the villagers.

FLUTTER!

In no time the man from the bank became buried under a pile of knickers.

"KNICKERS!" he cried.

As the knickers rained down, the villagers began to

realise what this Big Top was made from!

"THEY LOOK LIKE MY
KNICKERS!"

"THOSE FRILLY ONES
ARE MINE!"

"THE PINK ONES LOOK
FAMILIAR!"

"THIS WHOLE TENT
IS MADE OF KNICKERS!"

"I HAD A PAIR STOLEN
FROM MY WASHING LINE!"

"ME TOO!"

"AND ME!"

"THEY
WERE MY FAVOURITE
PAIR!" said the vicar. "RUINED!"

"BLUNDERS! GIVE US OUR
KNICKERS BACK!"

"YOU BLUNDERS
NICKED OUR KNICKERS!"

"THE PHANTOM KNICKER
THIEVES HAVE BEEN
UNMASKED!"

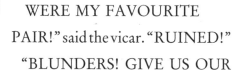

Just as a KNICKER RIOT was about to break out on the lawn, the ground began to shake.

GRUMPLE!

"EARTHQUAKE!" shouted the vicar.

But this was no earthquake.

VI

IT COULDN'T BE!
IT WOULDN'T BE!
IT SHOULDN'T BE!

IT WAS!
A HIPPOPOTAMUS!
Not just a hippopotamus,
A GALLOPING
HIPPOPOTAMUS!
Not just a galloping
hippopotamus,
A GALLOPING
HIPPOPOTAMUS
WITH AN OLD
LADY RIDING IT,
BRANDISHING A
BLUNDERBUSS!

"LADIES AND GENTLEMEN!

BOYS AND GIRLS!" cried Betsy, a pair of knickers on her head. "PLEASE TAKE YOUR SEATS! IT'S TIME FOR THE GRAND FINALE OF THE BLUNDER CIRCUS! OLD LADY BLUNDER AND A RHINOCEROS!"

"HIPPOPOTAMUS!" said Old Lady Blunder.

"HIPPOPOTAMUS!"

"That's what the smell of doobries was!" said Bunny to her brother. "Hippo doobries!"

"No doobry, Sherlock!" he replied.

Of course, no one took their seats. Not that they could have found them under the mountain of knickers. It was time to RUN, RUN, RUN FOR THEIR LIVES! (Making sure they had the correct knickers with them.)

"ARGH!"

"HELP!"

"RUN!"

"THOSE ARE MY KNICKERS!"

"NO! THEY'RE MINE!"

Only the man from the bank remained, still fighting his way out of the pile of knickers with the help of the policemen.

"WHOA, GIGI!" cried Old Lady Blunder, coming to a halt on the galloping hippopotamus.

"Where on earth did you get that hippo, Grandmamamamamamamama?" asked Bunny.

"I stole, I mean *borrowed*, Gigi from the local zoo!"

"HONK!"

"I love her!" said Bunny, patting her side.

Cedric was not so sure. He circled this interloper, squawking.

"SQUAWK!"

"Such a shame Gigi didn't get a chance to do her tap dance!"

"HONK!" agreed Gigi.

Finally, the man from the bank emerged from under the knickers.

He checked the time on his gold pocket watch.

"It's midnight!" he announced. "Blunders! Your time is up! Blunder Hall now belongs to the bank! You must leave immediately! Or you will be arrested!"

The Blunders looked at each other, aghast!

VII

"We Blunders will do no such thing!" cried Old Lady Blunder, still astride the hippopotamus. "You are forgetting all the money we made tonight from the Blunder Circus!"

All eyes turned to Betsy.

"Oh! I knew I had forgotten something!" she said.

"You didn't collect a penny, did you?" said the man from the bank.

She shook her head, her eyes glistening with tears.

"I am so ashamed!"

"Don't worry, darling!" said Bertie. "We all still love you! It was me who got us in this mess in the first place!"

"What an idiotic family you Blunders are," sneered the man from the bank.

"It's all here in black and white," he said, waving the contract. "These police constables are here to enforce it! This house will now become Blunder Borstal!"

"WE WILL NEVER LEAVE BLUNDER HALL!" cried Old Lady Blunder.

"Please!" pleaded Bunny. "Let us stay. This is our home!"

"And we have nowhere else to go," added Betsy.

"BOO! HOO! HOO!" replied the man from the bank, with deadly sarcasm. "Nothing and nobody can save you now!"

Fortunately, he was wrong.

Because at that moment Cedric stopped circling Gigi. He stood at the hippopotamus's ample bottom. The ostrich did what he often did to bottoms. He pecked it!

PECK!

"HOOOOOOOOOOOOONK!" honked the hippo.

Gigi broke into a gallop with Old Lady Blunder holding on for dear life.

"GIGI! STOP!"

But Gigi didn't stop. She galloped straight towards the man from the bank.

"NOO!" he cried, frozen to the spot in terror.

The policemen dived out of the way, and Butler made a running jump.

WHOMP!

He landed on top of the man from the bank, rolling him out of danger.

THOMP!

The pair hit the ground as Gigi galloped past. They missed being trampled by a whisker.

"GET OFF ME!" shouted the man from the bank as Butler lay on top of him.

"I was only trying to save your life, sir!" replied Butler.

"Well, next time, don't!"

"With pleasure, sir."

"ARREST THEM! ARREST THEM ALL! INCLUDING THE HIPPOPOTAMUS!"

"STOP! GIGI! STOP!" cried Old Lady Blunder.

To try to make the hippo halt, she fired her blunderbuss into the air.

BANG!

This had the opposite effect.

" H O O O O O O O O O O O O O O O O O O O O O O O O O N K ! "

Gigi bucked and charged straight towards Blunder Hall!

VIII

The hippo smashed
through the outside wall
into the dining room.

THEROMP!

"HONK!"

Then she burst through
the dining room wall
into the ballroom.

SMASH!

"HONK!"

Then she burst through
the ballroom wall
into the kitchen.

SMASH!

"HONK!"

There was no
stopping her!

Then she burst through

the kitchen wall and ended up back outside.

SMASH!

"HONK!"

"GIGI! I COMMAND YOU TO STOP!" cried Old Lady Blunder, now coated in a thick layer of dust.

She fired her blunderbuss again.

BANG!

The hippo ran riot! Old Lady Blunder fell to the ground...

THOMP!

...and scurried out of the way.

One by one, every wall in the house was destroyed.

SMASH!

"HONK!"

SMASH!

"HONK!"

SMASH!

"HONK!"

"PLEASE! STOP!"
cried the Blunders,
but the hippopotamus
wasn't listening.

Blunder Hall was
rumbling.

FURUMBLE!
The house began crumbling.

KERUMBLE!
The bricks started tumbling.

DERUMBLE!
All the Blunders,
Butler, Cedric and
the man from the
bank could do was
watch in horror
as Blunder Hall
collapsed to the
ground!

369

Blunder Hall had once been one of the greatest stately homes of England. Now it was a pile of rubble.

IX

Bunny burst into tears.

"NOOOO!"

"Oh, Bertie! What are we going to do?" asked Betsy.

"About what?"

"BLUNDER HALL FALLING DOWN!"

"Oh yes, yes, of course. That. I'm sad to say I don't think there is a thing we can do. Our beloved family home is no more."

Brutus turned to the man from the bank. "Well, at least you can't turn it into Blunder Borstal now, can you?"

The man was frothing with fury. "NO! Now it's worthless! WORTHLESS!"

He tore up the contract into a hundred tiny pieces and threw them in the air. They drifted down to the ground like confetti.

He stalked over to the hippopotamus.

"THIS IS ALL YOUR FAULT! YOU STUPID ANIMAL!"

The hippopotamus did not take kindly to this.

"HONK!"

Her ears twitched, her eyes narrowed and her nostrils flared.

She turned round and paced towards the man from the bank. Discreetly, the policemen stepped out of the way.

"Well, I didn't mean 'stupid'," he spluttered as the animal advanced upon him. He backed away, then broke into a run.

"NOOO!" he cried as Gigi gave chase.

"HONK! HONK! HONK!"

"ARGH!" he screamed as he fled. Just as he was about to dive into his Bentley, Gigi stomped on the car.

THONK! THANK! THUNK!

Now it looked as if it had been steamrollered.

The man from the bank hurled his bowler hat to the ground and jumped up and down on it.

"NO! NO! NO!" he cried. "I AM RUINED! RUINED!"

He put his now-flat hat on his head, much to the amusement of everyone else.

"HA! HA!"

"SQUAWK!"

"HONK!"

Humiliated, the man stomped off through the tall gates. Never to be seen again.

"Thank you, Blunders, for a most entertaining evening," said one of the policemen.

"But no more stealing knickers, please," said the other.

"We promise," replied the Blunders.

"Very good!"

With that, the pair marched down the drive, passing Gigi, who was coming back the other way.

"Well, Blunders," began Butler, "I suppose this is the end of my time as your butler!"

"What do you mean?" said Betsy. "You are as much a part of the family as Pegasus!" she added, patting the imaginary horse's flank.

"And families stick together," added Bertie. "Through good times **and** bad."

"It doesn't get much worse than this," said Bunny.

"Well, at least we now have a pile of rubble to play on," replied Brutus.

This set their mother off. Through tears, she said, "Oh! Whatever will we do?"

"I KNOW WHAT WE BLUNDERS WILL DO!" said Old Lady Blunder. "WE WILL REBUILD OUR BEAUTIFUL HOME! BRICK BY

BRICK BY BRICK! BLUNDER TO BLUNDER!"

"With a new hippo wing for Gigi!" exclaimed Bunny.

"HONK!" the hippo agreed.

Cedric was not so sure. He shook his head and squawked.

"SQUAWK!"

Betsy was sniffing back her tears. "But we Blunders have nothing. Nothing. Nothing at all."

"You are quite wrong, dear," replied Bertie. "We have everything. Because we have each other."

Without another word, Old Lady Blunder, Bertie, Betsy, Bunny, Brutus and Cedric came together for a Blunder family cuddle. Gigi nuzzled in too.

"And you, Butler!" said Bertie.

Smiling, Butler joined the cuddle too.

"Blunders! I love you all so much," said Bertie.

"And we all love you," replied the family.

Only Brutus didn't join in. Instead, he said,

"I think I'm going to puke!"

THE END

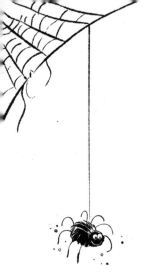